Praise for *Ye*

"A timely Columbus story without Columbus, a medieval fantasy that combines nuns, a genie, the New World, Prester John, and the end of all magic for a sharply, satisfying satiric romp."
—Carolyn Cushman, *Locus*

"An unusual and fascinating new direction for this writer, and a hauntingly strange story."
—*Science Fiction Chronicle*

"Both comedy and tragedy, with just enough hope at the end."
—*Feminist Bookstore News*

"Unique, highly irreverent but extremely humorous . . . Long in creativity and imagination."
—*Rave Reviews*

"A short and entertaining variant on this season's bounty of books dealing with the voyage of Columbus . . . Friesner's fast-moving tale dances a thin line between comedy and historical fatalism."
—*Newsday*

"Well, we all know what sort of story Esther M. Friesner writes. Comedy, right? The new Thorne Smith, perhaps, though she has more bite than he ever managed. But that's not all she *can* write, as she proves with *Yesterday We Saw Mermaids*."
—*Analog*

YESTERDAY WE SAW MERMAIDS

Esther M. Friesner

TOR
fantasy

A TOM DOHERTY ASSOCIATES BOOK
NEW YORK

First published 1993 as a Tor Book by
Tom Doherty Associates, Inc., New York

First published in Great Britain 1994 by Pan Books Limited
a division of Pan Macmillan Publishers Limited
Cavaye Place London SW10 9PG
and Basingstoke

Associated companies throughout the world

ISBN 0 330 33450 6
Copyright © Esther M. Friesner 1993

1 3 5 7 9 8 6 4 2

A CIP catalogue record for this book is available from
the British Library

Printed and bound in Great Britain by
Cox & Wyman Ltd, Reading, Berkshire

Dedicated to the memory of Dr. Isaac Asimov, a true discoverer of new worlds.

YESTERDAY WE SAW MERMAIDS

One

Yesterday we saw mermaids. Mother Catalina saw them first, just off the starboard bow of the brazen ship, and took it as a sign from God. I am not in the least surprised. To hear her tell it, we have been in the Savior's pouch ever since we left the convent of *las Descalzas de la Sangre Santa* in Palos, not three weeks since. Why should we escape it now?

The mermaids were a glorious sight. We first beheld them sporting amid a riot of dolphins, which the little Jewess insists are a harbinger of land—the dolphins, not the mermaids. Her prediction was notable for being the only optimistic divination she has made for the entire length of our unwished-for journey. Until the advent of our mermaids, every occurrence that the Jewess marked as an omen was invariably a dark one. Worse, all her grim foreseeings have come true. I cannot say what further disasters the appearance of the seafolk prognosticate, but I am certain it will be something either messy or nasty. *They* were both, God knows.

Seafolk or dolphins, present landfall or eventual death

in these unknown waters, I must be more careful of my words. These may be all that survives to speak of our fate if we do not return to Castile. Nun or liar, I must write this down.

The mermaids: They were not as lovely as the legends would lead one to expect, those strange people of the ocean-sea, and entirely unmusical, and far less courteous. They caught sight of us at about the same time that we first spied them, and they promptly abandoned the dolphins to their own devices. This alien water around us, of richest tourmaline hue, they churned into a snowy froth, so eager were they to reach our vessel.

The foremost among them seized hold of the few fishing lines that the Jewess watches over each day, the laggards making what progress they could up the ship's apparently smooth flanks. God and His Son alone know how the wicked creatures gained toeholds on what—to my eyes—is pure burnished metal! By devil-aided agility and unholy purpose, they swarmed up the sides and flung themselves into our midst on the foredeck. Sister Angustias screamed and fainted. She tends to do that rather too regularly for my taste. Even given the circumstances. . . .

I am beginning to think that *la Zagala* was right in the first place. Maybe Sister Angustias *would* be happier overboard, and thence to Heaven. But still, patience. *La Zagala* is but a gypsy wench, for all her powers. We are some of us more conventional Christians.

No sooner did the first of the mermaids set foot upon the deck, but Mother Catalina spread wide the full sheets of her habit and sailed forward to greet them in Christ's name. I remained behind, of course, together with the

Jewess and *la Zagala* and the lady Rasha of the Thousand Doors. Nor should Sister Angustias be forgotten, for she did remain above with us, though insensible. The other three nuns from our convent and Brother Garcilaso are somewhat lacking in faith, though I blush to record such shame of our confessor. They fled below so quickly at the mermaids' advent that it was as if they were water and the solid brass of the deck had turned into a sieve beneath them.

Ah yes, just as well. Brother Garcilaso would not have wished me to record his reactions had he lingered when the seafolk came aboard. No need to guess the greater shame, then; none.

The seafolk paid no mind to those of our company that huddled under hatches. They rushed up the plankless deck, straight for Mother Catalina. "Welcome, welcome, my children, in the name of the Blessed Virgin! Kneel down and receive the word of God, for to this end have His angels brought us unto you!" She opened her arms, as if to embrace them. I never saw her seamed and sun-starved face so blissful, so benevolent, save only when she was called upon to describe the torments of Hell to some poor novice wavering in her calling.

They did not kneel, nor give any sign of slowing; no, not in the name of however so many saints and martyrs. Without slackening their pace, they broke like a wave before the squat, black rock of Mother Catalina and flowed on to either side. They left her standing there with empty arms and vacant smile, like a draggled blackbird left afloat on a flood-uprooted tree.

Finely formed they were, even if not of the same mold

as Adam. Male and female too—I must not call them mer*maids* any more, less inexact habit of words breed inaccuracy, and then where is truth? For fully the half of them were furnished after the manner of men, and as the entire complement of them were naked as the eggs that hatched them, there was no denying what I saw.

"Mother of God!" I heard *la Zagala* exclaim as four of their vanguard came running slap-foot to where we stood. "I've seen black bulls with poorer pikestaffs!" And she swung her hips at them most indecently.

I felt the little Jewess cowering at my side. She claims to be virgin; let her. She still wore her yellow *sanbenito*, covered with its caricatures of prancing devils in eternal flame. Poor thing, she will taste the fire soon enough. Our present situation only gives her a temporary respite from what surely awaits all her kind. The sun rises in the east, a woman's place is by the fireside, and a Jew must burn: Thus the rule of Nature. Thus too the unassailable preachment of Brother Garcilaso, and therefore he has refused all petitions to permit the girl a change of dress.

Vengeance is the Lord's. In Brother Garcilaso's despite, I have read *that* much for myself. Knowing this, I did not feel quite so wrong to lay a comforting hand on the little Jewess' shoulder. (I do not wholly care for Brother Garcilaso.) "Don't be afraid," I told her. "God will protect our virtue."

"But whose God?" I heard the lady Rasha murmur through her veils.

And, "Virtue?" from *la Zagala*, just before her husky voice shattered with ribald laughter.

Ah no, a true lady never should travel with gypsies, given the choice.

Oh, how brightly the sun shines in these latitudes! My eyes were dazzled by its beams that chipped diamond sparks from the heaven-blue scales armoring our boarders. They were all around us. Plumy fringes colored a delicate carmine fronded up beneath their chins. The small breasts of the females were a paler tint than their scales, and covered with a tender down that held a myriad beads of water glimmering. What I first thought were seaweeds sleeking over their heads were in truth the rich ropes of their hair, elaborately braided and flowered with bits of shell. Male and female both lacked navel and nipples.

Mother Catalina stood dejected and ignored, with more than two-thirds of the deck to herself. Those merfolk that did not surround us, merrily clambered up the rigging. None of them had fishtails, but their extremities were overlong, webbed like a duck's feet. One of the males conquered the upper rigging and launched a rainbow spray of urine from the yardarm into the sea. A shame none fell on Sister Angustias. *That* would have been an awakening!

"What do you want?" the lady Rasha asked the creature nearest her. His tapering fingers were remarkably flexible and clever, her layered veils providing them with endless occupation. She slapped at his pryings and pluckings ineffectively, punctuating every tip-tap of her dark brown hands with small, shrill yippings, like her Moorish menfolk's battle cries.

"King Ferdinand's balls!" *la Zagala* exclaimed (and

13

only God's word that I bear true witness lets me commit such speech to writing!). "Here, girl, if you don't want a man to have you, put it so he understands." So saying, the gypsy wench kilted up her draggled skirt and with a sweep of her bare leg wedged one heel firmly at the juncture of the merman's lower limbs. Truly he was in this close kin to Adam after all, for he doubled over and rolled across the deck in anguish. Thick burblings escaped his mouth, plump blue lips pursed up as if for kisses.

Mother Catalina darted in like a swallow to offer him the word of God while he could not escape it.

Too late, too late. In death alone shall we learn how many souls *la Zagala's* ill-thought lesson cost us. The other merfolk saw their comrade fall and did not bide to see more. They scattered like spray dashed hard against the rocks. For a few moments, the air was a scaly flash of arcing bodies. The one who had conquered our yardarm leaped high against the sun before his body bent like an archer's bow and plummeted deep and cold into our wake. Even the injured one managed to thrust himself away from Mother Catalina's insistent salvation, slither through the railing, and tumble into the waves. The foam to both sides of our ship devoured them. I watched them plunge beneath the surface and vanish as completely as a dream.

The little Jewess ran to the golden rail, straining for one last glimpse. Her hair lashed out behind her, black and silken as the accursed banner of the Moors. I saw her tears. That makes four fools among us. I count myself.

I went to revive Sister Angustias, mentally cursing the besotted Genoese meddler whose wild rantings of new worlds had brought us all to this.

Two

I will kill Sister Angustias. No matter the penance, I will. Two days of her yammerings is one and a half days more than any soul should bear and still claim sanity. All up and down the decks she paces, wringing her hands as if she means to grind her pearl rosary to powder between her palms.

"Woe, we are doomed!" she cries. And again: "This is our punishment for consorting with heretics, devils, and curs!"

No doubt which classification she reserves for me. Back home in Palos, in the convent, she made it plain whenever opportunity presented that she was not in the habit of consorting with bastards, even those as richly dowered to *las Descalzas* as I. No one in *her* family was ever illegitimate. All the many generations of warriors that the Gutierrez clan sent out to fight the Moors, from the battle of Covadonga down to the final siege of Granada, remained strictly celibate in the field. Even when they embraced their wives, it was only because God so ordered.

I have seen Sister Angustias' mother. It would take a divine command.

Sister Angustias' endless pacing wears on the nerves. Though the wind holds fair for the west and the ship's swiftness slacks not, there has been nothing on our horizon since the merfolk came and went three days ago. That for the little Jewess' prophecies of land. She sees clearly in a dark crystal, else not at all.

On the afterdeck, the lady Rasha holds court beneath an awning of purple silk. Unless she summons one of us, her only attendants are *la Zagala* and the little Jewess. I watch as she dips her hennaed fingers betimes into a glazed earthenware pot of preserved apricots. Heaven knows where she gets them; the galley yields only rice and beans to us, but she dines on tender lamb, on artfully spiced forcemeat, on crisp-skinned fowl in a sauce of honey and slivered almonds. The smell of the gooey sweetmeats is strong. It overwhelms every other aroma in the deck's compass, save the scent of the sea itself, and the personal effluence of Brother Garcilaso.

Mother Catalina claims the foredeck as her province, and keeps us all ranged around her. We are supposed to be praying, but no one yet has taken it upon themselves to make me cease my scribbling this morning. Brother Garcilaso tried it towards the beginning of our voyage; once. The lady Rasha merely rubbed the side of her sweetmeat jar.

I do not know what to name the demon who emerged, the killing gray of a thunderhead starred over with stray bits of candied fruit, but it was a well-spoken fiend. Though no word of Christian Spanish escaped its red-tusked mouth, by the time it dwindled back into the lady Rasha's jar, it managed to make its wishes clearly understood: An honest scribe is not to be thwarted. The lady Rasha of the Thousand Doors interpreted the eloquent growlings and shakings and clawings Brother Garcilaso got from her pet horror very prettily (she speaks Castilian with an unfortunate southern lisp), just so that no one need question the order of things aboard her ship in future.

So it seems I am by default and diabolical will a scribe. Perhaps that makes me by association a devil as well as a cur.

Sister Angustias has crossed the deck from Mother Catalina's camp to the lady Rasha's realm forty-seven times so far. I keep track by making little tick-marks in the margin of this manuscript. There is little else to observe or note this day, in this heat. The beaten brass must be baking the soles from her feet. We are *las Descalzas,* a barefoot order, but even with the fine leather slippers Sister Angustias has always been allowed (three gemmed reliquaries and one of Saint Eulalia's wisdom teeth for the right foot, a pearl-sewn robe for Our Lady of Sorrows for the left), it must be scorching.

I have already exhausted all the evil names I ever knew to excoriate the mad mariner Colón. What good—save the Pope's word—can ever come to Spain out of Italy? I miss the merfolk. My mind wanders, and I see that soon this page will be filled with my poor sketches of Mother Catalina and Brother Garcilaso as a pair of bird-footed grotesques, or grit for an impossible dragon's craw. At least when there is no more room to write, I shall have some entertainment.

It is very puzzling, but every time I finish a leaf of parchment, I am under strict instructions to convey it to the lady Rasha, who stuffs it into her fruit jar. There comes a pause, then a many-timbred rumbling like laughter or complaint. The lady smiles or frowns accordingly, interpreting the humor of what dwells within the jar. My efforts have varying effects on the beast, it seems. So be it: In my brief life I have dealt with many critics.

Never a line nor a scrap of what goes into the jar ever comes out again; all is devoured. I soothe any misgivings I feel for the fate of my work by assuming that all my text is not in fact destroyed, but merely conveyed elsewhere. A jar that so well preserves fiends and apricots must treat the written word with some small courtesy!

After all, I am the demon-blessed scribe.

I wonder that the lady Rasha so lightly risks inserting her fingers into so chancy a hold, though. Once, as I watched her cram my finished parchment home, a ring slipped in from her hand. It was a yellow diamond as big as a swallow's egg, but she only tipped the jar over into her lap as though it were an ordinary vessel. The ring plopped out, sticky with syrup, a plump apricot wedged through its center. She offered the sweetmeat to me, which favor I declined. Would it have had the same savor on the tongue as earthly fruit? Or would there be a lingering tang of lost Eden's offerings awaiting me beneath the sugared skin? It is often noised that only those things around which we can close our lips can truly open our eyes.

I may never know. At times I regret that forfeited taste of enchantment. I fear my life has been an endless pilgrimage from one denial's shrine to the next. And will the pilgrim's palm I win at journey's end be a feast for my soul green and glorious enough to atone for all the fasts and vigils of my earthbound self?

Have I truly written such things down? Suchlike musings may yet cause me to merit the title of heretic, too, the last of Sister Angustias' anathematized trinity. Better I should have limned some more grotesques. Nor have I any hope of scraping clean the parchment. No one shall thwart the scribe, least of all the scribe herself. In ink there waits eternity. There's something for the lady Rasha's captive nightmare to chew on, at any rate. This page is done.

Three

No matter how many parchments my pen devours, no sooner is one in the jar than a fresh sheet always awaits me at *la Zagala*'s hand. The gypsy's grin is whiter than sun-bleached linen, even though the lady Rasha's skin is the darker and her teeth ought therefore to be the brighter by contrast. Perhaps it is the princess' diet. (Too many sweets will ruin a young woman's comeliness, as my noble father always said. May he burn.) Apart from its supernal gleam, there is too much *knowing* behind *la Zagala*'s smile to leave me tranquil. Neither she nor the lady Rasha will tell me whence proceed the empty parchments. I never see them until they are there, in the gypsy's hand. I do not even attempt to learn why the level in my inkwell remains the same.

My pens are my sanity. At least I know where they came from, though I have no idea what I shall do when they are gone. These are quills I find for myself, gray and white feathers shed weeks ago from the wings of seabirds. I laid in a fine supply when we were first airborne, scudding through the high clouds off the coast of Africa.

When the brazen ship made its initial leap into the sky, we encountered a flock of smoke-winged gulls. Pragmatic birds, they only saw our advent as a God-given chance to rest in midflight. They glided down to roost on the yards and railings. They did not leave our company until the ship reached the apex of her climb and began the slow downward coast back to the welcoming sea.

It was while Mother Catalina set me to work scrubbing birdlime from the decks that I managed to collect so many feathers. I sharpen them with my little knife, my mother's gift. No longer do I play that it is a sword.

Let me not think of my mother, dead, and treated as less than living while she died. (Illness too robs a woman of her comeliness, my father would say, and her utility in a man's bed.) I drove the memory of her face from my mind years ago, when the gates of *las Descalzas* slammed behind me. Only once did I call it back, in a moment whose like I shall never know again.

That is a day past all forgetting, and yet its first hours unrolled themselves like many others, gray and tedious, the dull trundling of the minutes accompanied by either the drone of our litanies or the slish-slish of the scrub brush on tile. It seemed to me then that I would spend all my life bowed over this basin of water or that, soapy or holy.

Our convent was once a Moorish merchant's home. More than two hundred years had passed since last the high-ceiled rooms sheltered any save consecrated virgins, yet still—how shall I say it and not be thought mad?— phantoms lingered. The mouths of the stone lions in the fountain courtyard trickled whispers as well as water.

When you bent over to scour the cool green tiles of the cloister clean enough to see your reflection, sometimes a second face would form itself from the snaky tangle of enigmatic characters baked firm into the bright ceramic surface. Kohl-rimmed eyes emphatically not your own would smile up at you from just behind your shoulder. When you turned to capture them, they were gone. The seldom breezes that blew through our cells all echoed the sound of gauze and damask flicking sharply around a plastered corner. Although our foundress impaled a holocaust of bleeding Christs upon the walls and sent a wave of whitewash crashing over every illicitly painted surface she could reach, she could not fully banish all the ghosts. At matins we still smelled blood oranges, at vespers our prayers were accompanied by an uninvited lute.

One would think that in two hundred years, our order might have learned to bear the unalterable and get on with the business of saving souls. In this, one would reck without Mother Catalina. Less than a week before that momentous morning, I was on my knees before the altar of the Assumption when I overheard her thick in ecstatic conspiracy with our confessor concerning the auto-da-fé.

"If we burn them here, Brother Garcilaso—our fountain court is large enough for so few heretics, I assure you—then the flames of the Holy Inquisition itself shall purify and bless our humble house once and for all."

"Are you still troubled by the witcheries, then?" I heard his words without any effort. Brother Garcilaso is one of those men who never lowers his voice for fear the world might miss something remarkable.

A sigh rocked Mother Catalina, a gust of regret strong

23

enough to make the altar candles gutter and drip wax over the Virgin's naked feet. "Still," she admitted, "I pray, I fast, I discipline the sisters; to no avail. Sister Incarnación swears she saw a lady veiled in saffron walk through the kitchen wall yesterday. *Saffron*, Brother Garcilaso! Did you ever hear the like?"

"Fear not." The sound of his hand patting hers was moist and fleshy. "Your time of trial is at an end. I shall speak to my brethren. The honor of expunging heresy from the holy bosom of Mother Spain shall be ours."

So it came to pass. I still recall the scandalized murmurs that gushed through the convent halls when the workmen arrived to build the scaffold and anchor the five stakes with their iron manacles. They were coarse, honest fellows, unemployed mariners from the port who bluntly voiced whatever was burdening their minds. We were forced to pass through the fountain court once or twice a day, and could not help but hear their opinions of us. Sister Angustias made complaint to Mother Catalina, blaming me for encouraging them with undue and immodest intimacy.

True, I had brought them watered wine without being so directed by Sister Cellaress, but the day was hot. Sister Cellaress, who is so sedulous in obtaining the choicest morsels for her rat-toothed lap dog, seemed convinced that workmen are kin to the angels, who require neither food nor drink to sustain them. So I took them wine, and Sister Angustias found out.

I think what galled my accuser more than my heterodox charity were the workmen's strident comparisons of our persons: She the sour-faced raven, I—truth before moot modesty—the soft-eyed dove. I soon had time to spare for contemplating my dove's eyes in another bucket of scrubwater. On the morning of the auto-da-fé, I found myself again on hands and knees beneath the cool marble colonnade ringing the fountain court.

God's ironies are manifold, reaching even beyond His mercies in sheer number. To witness the auto-da-fé was deemed a special indulgence, an honor reserved for those nuns whose spiritual perfections *almost* came near to satisfying Mother Catalina's exigent standards. Sister Angustias was among the chosen, of course, as were Sister Incarnación, Sister Elena, and Sister Magdalena. The rest of the conventual populace was remanded to the most secure enclosure for the duration of the ceremonies. By rights I should have shared their banishment. Instead, excused and shielded by my penitential bucket, I had my choice of view. Ignominy would appear to have its rewards.

No one noticed me, an insignificant tousle of soot-colored robes in the shelter of the delicately carven pillars. My duty set me right behind the benches provided for the civil authorities and the nobility who would attend. Mother Catalina and her favored brood occupied similar places directly across the courtyard, with Brother Garcilaso and a handful of his fellow Franciscans standing nearby to do what was requisite for the condemned, in the Church's name.

I wonder whether anyone thought to praise the foresight of the long-departed Moor who built our convent? Had he been less prosperous or less open-handed, *las Descalzas* should have been cheated of hosting this spectacle. The scaffold was equitably located equidistant from Church and lay witnesses, yet not near enough to either the lion fountain itself or any part of the surrounding convent proper for the blaze, once kindled, to imperil Christian holdings. We might without qualm observe the heretics die.

I could not. God, in His wisdom, neglected to give me so devout a heart. I saw them too closely as they were led into the courtyard. They were a family—if not by birth or by faith, then made one by shared adversity. Most striking of the five condemned were two old men whose snowy beards and age-garnered wisdom had not been enough to spare them the indignities and agonies of interrogation. It was a miracle that the Holy Office had not bilked itself of their exemplary demise. To be so old, to bear so much, and live! Their bones had been broken, their tendons torn, their muscles stretched like leather on a drying rack. They could barely stumble forward to the foot of the scaffold without the aid of the young man and woman who shouldered their negligible weight.

They—the couple I have mentioned—were in little better case. You could see the mottling of bruises overspreading faces otherwise handsome. Were they husband and wife? Brother and sister? Lover and beloved or merely total strangers who even now might not know by what name to call their companions? In the scant few breaths of life yet allotted them, such distinctions lost meaning. If they were in pain, they turned brave faces to it. They were not entirely certain on their feet, but youth lent them one last burst of strength that age denied. They used it to serve their elders.

The fifth of their group was a child. No, not a child—that is but the impression I had at first glimpse of her. The yellow swath of her *sanbenito* overwhelmed her small person. She walked behind the other four alone, apart, eyes downcast.

The young couple did not turn to her for any aid in helping the old men onto the scaffold. As I got to my feet and stealthily glanced between the intervening heads of the lay spectators, I saw her shoulders shake as with sobs. Her hands, manacled and chained to her loosely linked ankles, perforce remained weighted down before her; she could not wipe the tears away. She mounted the scaffold on her own, reluctant yet nimble as her fetters allowed, with no apparent pain to hinder her. It was then I read her riddle: She had not awaited the Question, but had confessed to all and everything the Holy Office might desire, so as to avoid our more persuasive methods.

It was as I realized this about the little Jewess that another odd revelation urged itself upon my senses. A perfume more penetrating than the sting of noble sweat came to me from the person of the man directly before me. Redolent of the altar—sweet beeswax tapers, honeyed frankincense—it was no scent that belonged to a layman. My overinquisitive nature betrayed me. Drawn forward by the intriguingly inapt aroma, I stumbled against its source.

He turned, likewise his companion. Did I gape? So I assume, for the lady's reaction was one of delighted wickedness. For the first time I beheld the black eyes and excellent white teeth of the infamous *la Zagala*. Her gypsy garb flared in a clash of brilliantly colored tatters, an assertive mongrel poverty so unbefitting the company of wealth and pure blood surrounding her that nothing natural could explain why no one save myself remarked it.

Ah, but I must deal with larger wonders. For *la Zagala*'s foreign splendor was swiftly rendered commonplace when I regarded her escort.

Not a man; I saw that now. Doublet, hose, and lavishly brocaded cote-hardie swam transparent above a gorgeous swirl of russet silk. Let fall a drop of ink into the waters of an enameled bowl and still you may discern the pattern beneath the tainted liquid. Just so the lady's superficial disguise of face, dress, sex, all wavered and thinned over the surface of her true self. Behind the regally bearded and sun-bronzed mask of a Spanish lord bided the veiled and gem-framed face of a highborn Moorish lady. Thus my initial introduction to the lady Rasha of the Thousand Doors.

With smiling eyes she observed my astonishment, then turned to the gypsy wench and asked, "This one, too?"

La Zagala's teeth flashed. "We must. She knows us. And who knows what more she sees? We must be grateful for Fortune's gifts, my lady. Much may be wanted on our voyage."

I comprehend nothing of her meaning, too rapt by the patent fact that no one else appeared to hear the gypsy's words.

"Allah witness, you speak truth." The lady sighed, and dropped a certain veil. She uncovered neither face nor form thereby, but merely revealed the tiny perfection of

a fully rigged ship which had remained shrouded beneath
a scrap of gold-shot samite until this.

I did not then have the power to question why the lady
held fast to such a toy. My mind was preoccupied with
more immediate terrors. What manner of women were
these, and what had brought them here? Could these be
the less timid sisters of our convent's ordinary manifesta-
tions? If black enchantment were afoot, that were cause
enough for panic, but how must it be compounded for me
since I alone of all those present could both see and hear
them! I did not know why God had chosen so to try me,
but I was certain that give Sister Angustias one whiff of
this knowledge and a sixth stake would be added to the
tally in the courtyard.

I am a coward. I fled. Brush and bucket flew with me
to the harbor of the facing colonnade where my sisters
waited and smiled and told their beads while the execu-
tioner adjusted the chains binding the five to their stakes.
As I flitted from shadow to shadow, I overheard our
confessor Brother Garcilaso chewing over a tasty bit of
gossip with one of his fellow Franciscans.

"From Palos, you say? And when?"

"This very day. She has given him three ships!"

Brother Garcilaso's tonsure mottled red with rage.
"Vile waste. Our order would make more practical use of
the funds thus squandered on that plague-rat Genoese!"
With an expansive gesture he described the courtyard's
compass, silently painting vistas of vaster, more lavishly
subsidized autos-da-fé.

His brother, a friar built like a granite mounting block,

lowered his voice almost past the point where my ears could hear him hiss, "Genoese . . . and Jew."

"*What!*"

The stocky friar hushed Brother Garcilaso with square, soft hands. "So rumor says. He resided at the monastery of *la Rábida* while awaiting word from Their Most Catholic Majesties. A cousin of mine serves there. There were—certain suspicions. The name Colón itself . . ." He let his voice drift off, the while looking privy to all mysteries. It was a deep disappointment to a well worked-up Brother Garcilaso when the second friar finished with: "But all that was entirely cleared up before any royal bequest was made. He is a good Christian, the Genoese; good enough for our kings' approval, and that is good enough for me. God grant he is also a good sailor, to find our sovereigns this precious western route to the Indies."

Brother Garcilaso's outrage was not so easily shunted aside. "A Jew!" he expostulated. "The horror, Brother Rodrigo! And if he should be successful in his voyage? A new path to the riches of the East in the hands of *those* people? For he would betray his trust, Brother, rely upon it. Traitors all, renegades, apostates! The perfidious Israelite would take the riches of Castile and Aragon, only to found a kingdom of the Jews shored up with the gold of Cipango!"

"A kingdom of the Jews. . . ." Brother Rodrigo's belly heaved with modest laughter. "What a notion. No, no, my dear Brother Garcilaso, you are not listening. It was rumor, nothing more. The Indies shall be Catholic Spain's and—God grant it—we shall bring them greater treasures than we take away."

Brother Garcilaso solemnly inclined his head. "The Word of God." He gave this weighty pronouncement the benison of silence, but soon lifted up his round little dumpling of a chin when a flicker of firelight at a torch's end signaled that the executioners were eager to administer the Word of God to the congregation of five in their own irrefutable way.

First, however, the sermons.

Two priests and a bishop went up upon the scaffold where the condemned stood chained for the flames. Each man of the Church took his turn to lay so many charges of treachery to the prisoners' collective account that had Judas been present, he might have been held up as an exemplum of highest virtue, if only by comparison. I would say that the clergy flayed the very skin from the prisoners' bodies, but for the suspicion I had that nigh all of the five had already received an analogous service in the concrete rather than the figurative sense.

Brother Garcilaso—

Four

Why is everyone so angry with me? It was not my fault. I only wrote what I had witnessed. Who would pay me for telling lies?

For that matter, who pays me for the truth?

I should be the one to take offense. Did I ask to be interrupted? Did I invite Brother Garcilaso to jab that bag-pudding chin of his over my shoulder and pry into words that did not concern him?

Could I guess he would take such umbrage at—think of it!—my description of that selfsame chin?

"See what falsehood the lazy creature scribbles!" he cried, tearing the unfinished page from beneath my pen and waving it overhead like the banner of a captured Moorish city. "May God forgive her for an idle sinner, a parasite upon the flesh of her more honest and industrious sisters!"

Sister Angustias paused in her endless pacings. She dropped her groans in favor of bright, eager, repetitive concurrence with our confessor's evaluation of my work. How fortunate that he had but a single page to hand (the rest already having been safely ruminated over by the lady Rasha's captive devil). I tremble to think of what Sister Angustias would make of my earlier analyses of her many virtues.

I tremble, but not with fear. Is it my imagination, or have I caught myself smiling—no, *grinning* like a sparrow-glutted cat!—more and more the farther the brazen ship takes us from Palos? I am growing wickeder by the day. I suppose I should regret it more.

Brother Garcilaso and Sister Angustias performed a fine part song, melody and descant, on the theme of my character. Ah, such a hue and cry my other sisters' conjoined voices set to then! Trained to sing in choir, how could they resist chiming in, point and counterpoint? I was sloth personified, a shirker who hid behind a shield of airy words while my betters did true labor. Mother Catalina lent her wholehearted approval to their song. Like the others, she saw fit to allow one fact in the case to elude her: They had none of them done anything more exhausting than pray and stitch, stitch and pray, since first we settled into life here aboard the brazen ship.

But facts are such confusing things.

Virtue offended, in truth or imagination, mounts a more hideous cacophony than a full hunting pack of the seven deadly sins. Not even when the lady Rasha rose from her divan and held out the earthenware jar with its encapsuled horror did they still their clamor. I saw anger storm the royal lady's brow, and her fingertips begin to stroke the drowsing fiend into full manifestation from his nest among the apricots.

It was the little Jewess stopped her. She laid one small

hand over the lady Rasha's jeweled fingers and said something in a voice so low that naturally I could not hear it—not with the full distance of the gleaming deck between us. The lady harked, then nodded. The little Jewess left her and *la Zagala*, crossing the deck to where we roosted in our somber plumage. Her hands were gracefully folded over the front of her billowing yellow *sanbenito*. She looked for all the world like one of my father's legitimate daughters on her way to Holy Mass.

Her approach caused Brother Garcilaso to burst into a spate of abuse and vilification shoddily underpropped by a smattering of Our Lord's teachings. Never has it been my privilege to hear Holy Writ so exuberantly misapplied, nor with such vigorous ignorance. Well, that is Brother Garcilaso for you. Infidels bring out the best in him.

The little Jewess was unmoved by the lowest epithets he selected for her. She waited until he had worked his complexion up into that florid state where a man must either pause to take breath or burst a blood vessel. Our luck was such that he chose the former course.

"Please give her back her writing, Brother," the little Jewess said. "The lady Rasha of the Thousand Doors would have you know that this time, the creature who serves her house will not bother to teach you a lesson. It will kill you outright."

Brother Garcilaso's absurd little chin rose haughtily, like a most aristocratic meatball. "I am the servant of the Lord," he said, "and I fear no servant of the Devil!"

"Your fear is of no consequence," the little Jewess replied in singularly reasonable tones. "It is all so simple: Give back the writing or you will die. Touch it again and you will die: Prevent her from writing and you will die. It is all your choice to make." She started back over the deck just as composed and self-possessed as when she had come. She paused midway.

"Disemboweled," she added. "I have seen it so in my visions. Your entrails will be punctured by the creature's talons and held up steaming before your face while you still live. The smell will be awful. You won't like it." She returned to her place without further commentary.

I had my sheet back before me while she had yet the better part of the deck to cross. May I be forgiven my sins, but I confess I refused to set pen to paper anymore that day. It was amusing to see how my recalcitrance put my confessor all of a state. I have only deigned to take up the pen again today for a little while in order to quiet his panicked shrillings, and Mother Catalina's sympathetic lowing on his behalf.

What is it about a scratching pen? It draws more unwanted attention than if I took off all my clothes and danced in the city plaza. Now it is the lady Rasha who chooses to perambulate the deck and just happens to pause behind me as I write.

"We do not need so much of your opinion, scribe," she says. "Nor your personal prejudices. Return to testimony, and recount only what you saw. You were describing the auto-da-fé—barbarous!—and I think you earlier mentioned your mother to some purpose. I would have you write. . . ." And her voice trails off, wandering among a hundred thousand hints that would surely make my tale all the better if only she were the one to tell it.

She never goes so far as to try writing it herself.

I will do as she suggests—or rather, commands. If I displease the demon in the jar, I need only listen to a few minutes' disconcerting growls. If I displease the lady Rasha, however—

It is her ship, and all our lives ride on it. A word from her, and it may vanish out from under our feet while she, *la Zagala*, and the little Jewess look to other resources. I am sure they have a few.

No, I do not think I will deliberately displease the lady Rasha. Not so long as my livelihood depends on her favor.

But neither will I write or not write other than what is in my heart.

Five

The sermons were done.

My eyes are good, and I was standing in the shade. Therefore it was no illusion when the last sermon was given, the executioners summonded to stand ready, and the prisoners actually exchanged unmistakable glances of relief. They knew they were to die, that it was inescapable. All they would request, were any to ask them, was that death now come quickly and be done with.

The way of the sinner is hard. Brother Garcilaso jumped from his place and scurried over to whisper urgently in the ear of a most gorgeously garbed official. Rings gemmed with emeralds and Baltic amber flashed imperiously in the sun. I knew those rings. I knew that man.

My father, don Ignacio Pelayo de Serra y Vasconcelos: Queen Isabela's man, lord of Montesinos castle, knight-*comendador* of the Order of Calatrava, rich, powerful, and most devout in the holy service of that worthiest divinity, his own desires. Sometimes, however, he felt it both convenient and expedient to cultivate the good graces of the Church. He had a passion for Franciscans, especially their excellent administrative abilities in aid of the Holy Office of the Inquisition.

He signaled, and the executioners paused. Coolly he nodded to Brother Garcilaso. It appeared that our confessor had something to say which would immeasurably enrich the forthcoming executions. The monk preened and puffed like a love-maddened pigeon, bowed more elaborately to my father than he ever bent the knee before any shrine, and mounted the platform to add his mouthful to the spew of words that had preceded him.

I do not think the fiend that the lady Rasha keeps within her tidbit jar will fully appreciate all the erudition and scholarship that went into Brother Garcilaso's speech. He had taken as his text Our Lord's bidding that if a man strike you on one cheek, you should turn him the other also. Though such vast libraries as the Franciscans ward are not the province of women, I have always been bold to interpret the Lord's words for myself. After fifteen minutes of Brother Garcilaso's exegesis, I discovered I had it all quite wrong. It seems that if a man strike you on one cheek, you turn him the other and while he has his hand drawn back for the second blow, you bare a dagger in God's name and stab him through the ribs.

Hallelujah.

I mean not to imply that Brother Garcilaso's sermon was other than entrancing, but after an additional twenty minutes I found my eyes beginning to wander. I glanced back across the courtyard, low curiosity urging me to spy out the reactions his speech was having on the secular powers.

Never did I see so much remorse pull down the waxy jowls of my father's face. I marvel that the strain of so unfamiliar an emotion did not wholly undo the man. He showed only a great easement when my mother died. I recall him all conviviality when he told me I was to enter *las Descalzas*. I knelt before him and begged leave to depart his house with the clothes on my back rather than lose my life between cramped convent walls; he heard the spring wind and greeted it with a gentle smile. If not for Brother Garcilaso's ongoing sermon, I might never have known the man capable of penitence. *What have I done?* his eyes seemed to wail. *Can there be absolution for a man who knowingly released this upon an unwitting world?* I thought he was like to cry.

There were other stirrings in the richly garbed ranks behind him. Whispers turned to murmurs, murmurs to grumblings of rebellion. I thought I saw someone on the farthest bench rise as if to leave, only to be quelled back into place by the gimlet eye of the bishop. If you cannot bear with sorrow, God will help you, but if you cannot bear with a churchman's oratory, the Holy Office might take sudden interest in your name.

Brother Garcilaso went on. He had managed to veer from stricken cheeks in want of turning to offending eyes and hands that demanded plucking out and chopping off, respectively. He had commenced the verbal immolation of whatever body parts were left when it happened.

"Enough!" cried *la Zagala*, rising from her place across the courtyard. "We can wait no longer and still have hopes of a decent tide." Her glamour was cast aside. She pushed her way through the stupefied crowd of witnesses. The lady Rasha followed, still wrapped in the illusion of masculinity. It was beginning to tatter at the edges, giving the people a startling sight: A towering Castilian nobleman with kohl-rimmed eyes and hennaed mouth; a belted warrior who minced his way between the benches and stools on tiny, sandaled feet.

"What blasphemy is this? What witchcraft?" Mother Catalina trilled. Her papery hands fluttered about her face. Nervous sweat stung its scent through her chosen wash of orange-flower water.

The courtyard was all agog, the Church in a discrete uproar, the laymen of no practical use. Words flew, but bodies remained where they were. Even the executioners seemed paralytic, and they are reputed to be the most phlegmatic of men. To this day I have been unable to learn whether the general immobility was the result of gypsy sorcery, Moorish enchantment, or merely the freezing mundanity of the unimaginative confronted by the unexpected.

Shall it be thought pride if I say that I was the first to regain some self-command? I raced around the colonnade, seeking the best vantage point. Oh, not for my soul's saving would I miss wink or blink of this! I found my desired sentry post beneath the shadow of the scaffold, from whence I might observe without myself being seen. Above my head Brother Garcilaso—now speechless, miracle!—still paced the boards. I clung to the centermost pole and peered out over the piled fagots.

The rag of samite whipped the air as the lady Rasha unveiled her miniature barque for the second time that day. Its brassy flanks caught the sun, reflected a blinding sheet of light into the already dazzled eyes of the massed clergy and their select flock. She tossed the tiny vessel into the air, as lightly and gracefully as if it were a clew of yarn. It sailed high, spinning on its rudder like a child's top, but otherwise remarkably steady as it climbed the blue.

The lady Rasha dropped all pretense of past masquerade and sang to the ship as it soared. Her magicked garments melted one by one, leaving her to stand before every eye in those exotic clothes that at once eloquently describe the female figure that they feign to hide. My own envious heart smote me to see how fair she was. Nothing so lovely could go unloved, for the world is all injustice. To be plain is to await death and gloat over the grave's harsh way with beauty.

I could not do that, not even if the lady Rasha had the art to steal from my memories the few insignificant moments of happiness I have known. Her beauty was not hard, like my father's gems, but warm and welcoming as an infant's hand that closes on your teasing finger as if to say, *There! You are all I want in this world. I will not let you go.*

The lady Rasha's voice was no less lovely than her person. She sang, and sorcery was done thereby. A tremble and an exaltation of alien melody cast golden threads of music onto the wind. Golden, I say, for I saw their sparkle materialize as each note became a precious strand, solidified beneath the keel of the twirling ship.

The lady sang: The filaments of sound made visible plaited themselves into strong hawsers that lost their flexibility as they changed from thread to rope to pillar of

43

sun-born stone, raising the ship up and up into the sky. A shadow spread slowly from beneath its curving metal sides, a shadow that grew as that which cast it grew. I hastened out from under the scaffold to make certain I was seeing rightly, even daring to come right into the fountain courtyard rather than remain in doubt and darkness.

Yes, it was so: The brass ship had grown from the size of a toy to the bulk of a goodly shallop, and as the lady Rasha's song raised it farther from the earth, it continued to burgeon in this unwonted fashion.

A flash of gaily colored skirts distracted my eye. I saw *la Zagala* streak past me and scale the scaffold monkey-nimble. Straight for the middle post she went and laid hands on the chains binding the little Jewess. They powdered at her touch. As soon as she had her free, the gypsy tried to drag her away, but the girl resisted. There was no hearing anything but the lady Rasha's song, yet I could see how the little Jewess clung to *la Zagala*'s hand as she begged her to give similar release to the four captives still in chains.

I saw the gypsy shake her head sadly, despite all the little Jewess' affecting petitions. When words would not serve her, the girl flung her arms around the neck of the other chained woman and made it plain that she would not go without her companions.

By this, the audience had recovered some measure of its wits. One miracle turns a man to stone; too many turn him back into animate clay. I suppose this is why you never hear of virgins overrun by herds of chastity-drunk unicorns: We best digest our wonders singly. The churchmen were the first to stir, being regular traffickers with the unearthly. I was unastonished to hear the bishop bellow for a sword, in God's name, no less to see my father spring to the fore, blade in hand, attentive to the wishes of the Church. He made straight for the scaffold.

Others turned their attention to the lady Rasha. Her music lacked the stunning power of the sirens' legended song, but that was not its purpose. Over her head the ship continued to grow, swollen with melody. It went from shallop size to cog, from cog to caravel before the lady chose to cease her first song. The sustaining pillar of gold beneath the vessel vanished. By now the fountain court-yard lay in shadow, only a sifting of sunlight able to slip through the barricade of the great ship hovering above.

I counted four great hulks of swordsmen who vaulted from their places, charged the lady with bare steel, and reined themselves back so sharply a blade's length from her person that the forerunners nearly ended as cold meat on the fine Toledos of those who loped after. I took this as further evidence of the Moorish lady's uncanny pow-ers. Now I realize that it was plain prudence caused the men to restrain their arms. If they should slay the lady whose song kept the enchanted ship afloat on high, what would be left to sustain it? They were not of an explora-tory or experimental nature, those men, and neither fear of Hell or the Holy Office would budge them. Let some-one else cut the Moor's throat as soon as they were safely far from where the ship might fall!

At the time, though, I thought it all very extraordinary and wondered why the lady did not divert a portion of this happy magic to shield her gypsy friend and the freed

Jewess from their own peril. My father, you see, showed no sign of relenting, or even of slowing. He was atop the scaffold and at them. He brandished his sword for *la Zagala*'s benefit as he enumerated all the moral lessons he meant to give the black wench who dared interfere with Christians.

He might have intended to frighten *la Zagala* and the little Jewess, to spice their inevitable deaths with some anticipatory terror. I recall how long he allowed me to grovel at his footstool, begging for any fate but the convent, before he went ahead and did exactly what he had planned to do from the first. My abasement did not swerve him, but he did find it amusing. Now he sought to evoke similar entertainment from the women on the platform through threats, bull-bawlings, and slicing the intervening air into streamers.

Poor Brother Garcilaso. He was standing right between my father and his prey. One look at the warrior's bluster and posturings was enough: The gypsy laughed, the monk fainted, the little Jewess automatically knelt to catch him, my father stepped forward to sever her head (and possibly Brother Garcilaso's; it *had* been such a long sermon), and I screamed.

My father jerked his head and saw me in the middle of the courtyard. His face darkened perceptibly, even in the shade of the brazen ship. The lady Rasha had changed her tune and was now humming a hypnotic monotone that made broad pennants of blue light unroll themselves from the ship's siderails. While my father roared uncounted curses at me for publicly disgracing him by such vulgar behavior, one of these bright gangways slid beneath the lady Rasha's dainty feet and elevated her gently to the deck. Her sweet continuo swelled as she mounted the air, echoed louder as she set foot aboard, and strength poured from her voice into the other unscrolling ribbons of light.

One snaked down to capture *la Zagala* and the little Jewess. When she saw what was happening, the girl tried to divest herself of our unconscious confessor and seize hold of her still captive comrades. Awash in the clean blue light, *la Zagala* broke the grip of the small hands knotted in the folds of another *sanbenito*. Four darts of crackling black fire shot from the gypsy's fingertips and spattered to starry flowers on the prisoners' brows. The little Jewess wailed as she saw them slump dead against their chains. Even my father lost color from his face and stared at *la Zagala* with respect and fear.

The gypsy could not have cared less for don Ignacio's respect. Her eyes were on the floating ship; her mind too, evidently, for she seized the little Jewess by the wrist without a backward glance and let the blue light uplift them.

I watched their ascent, thinking how badly the wench would be surprised when she saw that her prize had taken a prize of her own: The cincture of Brother Garcilaso's habit had tangled around the little Jewess' ankle when they lay tumbled together on the scaffold. He hung doubled over from that twisted leash, dangling like a slaughtered sheep. When he achieved a certain altitude it was fully possible to view from below the monk's generous hams. Some of our confessor's fellow churchmen fell to their knees, crying miracle; others howled for all the saints to save the poor man from the snares of witchery.

The bishop looked undecided between impotent outrage and helpless laughter.

I knew my choice, if such it was. Had I any choice but one, with so inspirational a vantage of Brother Garcilaso's rosy nether smile rising ever higher above me? I laughed until my face was wet with tears. I laughed until the bodily aches of constant convent labor were lost in the joyful throbbing of my ribcage. I laughed until I no longer knew there was such a place as this miserable cage in the heart of Palos or such a person as the castoff bastard pawn, myself, Sister Ana Teresa de Serra e Hita.

Alas, I also laughed so hard that I never noticed the cloak of blue light falling over my coarse habit until ten hard fingers dug deep into my shoulders and a hatefully familiar voice shrieked in triumph, "I have her, Mother! I have her, *Comendador!*" I wiped the tears from my eyes and saw Sister Angustias, sky blue, leering merrily in my face as she crowed, "Now you'll dance."

Then all too many things happened at once, and the only one I can be sure of—for I have been most scrupulous over the truth in these humble writings—is that I gave Sister Angustias forceful and immediate opportunity to practice Brother Garcilaso's lesson on turning the other cheek.

Six

I heard my hand strike her face with a sound like a wooden trencher hitting a stone floor. I heard her cry out, though to her dogged credit she never loosed her hold on my habit. I heard Mother Catalina and the other nuns explode into a riot of confused reactions, doves when the weasel breaches the cote doors.

Their voices grew louder and louder; I could not then think why. The light was too strong around me, blurring my sight, bringing visions. The courtyard stones dropped from beneath my feet. The utter strangeness of that sensation ravished all anxiety from my heart. I heard many screams, but knew none of them for mine. There was no wind on my face, only a gradual lightening that enveloped me, like shedding winter cloaks one by one, or coming to the surface from deep water. I recall wishing that Sister Angustias would not drive her nails so painfully into my skin, nor drag down so hard on my shoulders. From a place far away came deeper-throated yammerings, and the acrid assault of burning wood.

That was when I saw my mother. Then, in the light, in

the air, on the pathways of the angels. She was robed in love and crowned with sweet serenity. The tears that came again as I stretched out my hands to touch her did not affect the cool perfection of her face. The look of blessing and affection she gave me was better than any smile. Her hands, clasped in silent worship when first seen, extended readily to meet mine. Her fingers were the cool benediction of rain.

Warm metal jarred up against my bare feet. My mother's apparition disappeared. I staggered backwards until a hard pole laid itself across my lower spine and I saw that I was on the deck of the brazen ship, the railing at my back. I do not think I wondered just yet about what had become of Sister Angustias' relentless grip. There was too much else to occupy my mind.

A short space away, *la Zagala* was glowering at the little Jewess, still embarrassed of her monkish burden. Beyond them, the lady Rasha paused, took breath, and gave a long, reveling ululation. The ship shuddered like a highbred horse, gathered itself together, and made one majestic, glorious, incredible leap against the sun.

The metal deck tilted crazily; my feet could get no purchase. I flailed for something to hold onto. No use: The angle of ascent was too steep. My feet slipped away and I skidded down the canted deck in an immodest sprawl of black wool, white linen, and more legs that I remembered having been born with. A thud as we all pitched up against the poop cabin, and I saw why.

"Get your feet out of my face," said Sister Magdalena.

She is one of the older members of *las Descalzas*, and has borne with Mother Catalina's rule longer than any of us. For this alone I honor her, though the shameless toadying she uses to survive will not let me respect her.

Most deferentially I stammered an apology, only to have her snap, "Not you, you little fool. It's Incarnación's great paws are smothering me!"

"Well, I like that!" came the rejoinder from somewhere to my right. A heap of dust-grayed habit humped itself erect and I saw Sister Incarnación's pinched and pale face peering down at me. She leaned hard against the poop cabin wall and smoothed her habit. "Find someone else to blame."

"I believe, my daughter, that the paws are mine." Mother Catalina shaped her speech in a cunning manner. The words were more self-effacing than any true saint's, yet her intonation of the same hummed with more unvoiced threats of revenge than a pride-stung Italian princeling.

"Get up, get up, get *up!*" Someone jabbed me where I blush to mention. One by one, like a tussle of puppies, my sisters and I disentangled ourselves. To the last woman, we had been so thoroughly aggravated by the buffeting dealt us in the ship's wild leap that mutual rancor unseated any other emotion. Clinging to one another we made a human chain that inched its way across the precipitously sloping deck to the siderails. There we clung and stared down into pure magic or pure madness.

No wave of water swelled beneath our keel. A fathomless abyss of empty sky rushed away from the brass ship's stern. Far behind us lay the smoke of the blaze from the courtyard fire where the little Jewess' kin were being consumed. *La Zagala* had cheated the Holy Office of the victims' final agony in the flames, but the bishop was a tidy man. No doubt he gave the order to proceed, both to preserve the solemnity of the occasion and his own illusion of control.

The courtyard, our convent, Palos itself dwindled rapidly to smears of white and green, brown and blue. Only the distant vista of the open sea retained some sense of its own grandeur. Though I could not see them rightly from that ever increasing height, I knew that far below us three small ships were clearing the mouth of Palos harbor. Three ships laden with arrogance and greed had cast off from their moorings within the same hour as our own had soared free. I imagined I could see the sailors squirreling up the rigging, the lordly new-made Admiral of the Ocean-Sea clasping the rail and doffing his velvet cap for the ladies.

"No, you didn't," says the lady Rasha, coming up to peek over my shoulder once more.

All right, I didn't. I wrote *imagined*, didn't I? Let her assume the duties of the pen, if she thinks she can do it better!

Seven

In the name of Allah, the All-Seeing, the Merciful, the Gracious, I, his unworthy daughter Rasha of the Thousand Doors do take pen and ink in hand, assuming for the most ungrateful, inconsiderate, impatient and unladylike—even for an idolatrous Unbeliever—Ana de Serra e Hita, called Sister, the holy and blessed task of immortalizing the tale of our divinely appointed and directed journey into the Outermost Western Reaches of the Great Sea.

May He who numbers the stars and is mindful of the disposition of the smallest dewdrop upon the wakening petals of the rose be now equally mindful of my humble efforts, and set His seal upon the true and veracious testimony which Fortune and my lord Zamiz the Unaccountably Repulsive have conspired to compel one of our company to render imperdurable, in the inharmonious and crude tongue of the Iberian savages. May he whose kingdom we seek likewise find it pleasing, when my lord Zamiz the Unaccountably Repulsive shall lay this record before him, so that he may look with favor upon us, his most humble petitioners, and grant us but a few grains of the mighty mountain of his powers.

Verily has the sage written—

I took the paper away from her. At the rate the lady Rasha writes, we might have tumbled off the lip of the world and she would still be wrangling with her God over grammar.

She seemed rather relieved when I reclaimed my abdicated post as scribe. The violent uproar that issued from her tidbit jar when she inserted her page-long effort convinced her further that her talents lay in other fields.

We have an agreement, now: She sings magic, I write facts.

We have also become friends.

The knowledge that his child, however illegitimate, has taken a Moor into her confidence would kill my father. Would there were some way for Zamiz the Unaccountably Repulsive to bring him the news.

But the fiend has other fish to fry. Friendship brings revelations, not all of them amusing or pleasant. At last I am privy to the purpose of this journey, and if my hand does not shake badly enough to send a shower of ink-blots over the page it is because I am by this resigned to my fate.

We were not part of the original plan. Our presence aboard this ship is all unhappy accident, start to finish, let Mother Catalina rave about God's will never so tirelessly. No provision was made for us. We shall reach land, and then we shall die.

Oh, Brother Garcilaso, if you only knew why we have

been snatched up from our sundry small lives to race against time and a Genoese lunatic for the western lands! Modest monk, have you never dreamed of wearing ecclesiastical garments that would transform you from pedant to prince of the Church? Did the temptation never move you to picture yourself lifted from your humble duties to officiate before an altar where precious stones and priceless metals outshine the glory of the Sacrament? Was there no reverie of your inmost heart in which you stood in splendor as the chiefest jewel within a cathedral whose choir stalls were porphyry, whose very windows were translucent sheets of slivered gems?

You must have. I know you. And alas, what the lady Rasha tells me is tantamount to saying you shall have your dream before too long. In its wake it shall bring you a rough and bloody awakening.

For we seek the kingdom of Prester John.

When we find it, we are like to die. How else might it be? Even I have heard of that legended priest-king's realm, so long, so futilely hunted down the centuries by adventurers and soldiers of fortune. Marvels are told of Prester John's riches, but what are wordly goods? The Holy Father behind the walls of Rome commands the wherewithal to purchase all Galilee, yet the Turks remain unimpressed. It is in the nature of his subjects and the power he possesses to tame them into approximate Christianity that the veritable marvel of Prester John's legend lies.

Yes, we shall die. I have seen enough of my father's reaction to uninvited callers to know this. Prester John did not send for us, nor have we legitimate claims upon

him, such as the lady Rasha's, to excuse our incursion.
With my luck, we shall arrive precisely as he sits down to
sup. If our doom be at the hands of his unearthly congregation or in the jaws of beasts out of legend and lore, I
cannot tell. But this I know: If we do not reach his kingdom before the fool Colón, things more wonderful than
we shall perish.

Eight

There is still no sight of land. Before, I might have felt some small anxiety over whether our stores should last out the voyage or if indeed the Ocean-Sea pours from the world's rim into the gulfs of night. Now, with all the lady Rasha has told me, a plunge into Tartarus seems preferable. Ignorance goes garbed in folly, but knowledge is worse than a hair shirt when worn next to the skin.

I know now that something does lie beyond the horizon: Something marvelous, something dread. The merfolk were its heralds, its most mischievous children who delight in straying far. The lady Rasha tells me that grander prodigies summon us, wonders to stun insensible the ordinary imagination.

Man-eating dragons are not the half of it, as the lady Rasha knows.

To ask how the lady Rasha knows this is to ask who is the lady Rasha. I will be brief: She is the bride of the creature in her jar, the fiend she names Zamiz the Unaccountably Repulsive.

She tells me that it is a great convenience for any lady

to have such a mate. Looks are not everything, and Zamiz is devoted to her. Too, he is quite content to remain in his jar, only appearing at his wife's bidding. I can see the benefits of this matrimonial arrangement.

The lady Rasha of the Thousand Doors was so named because her beauty dictated prudence to a father who was reputed to drive the hardest bargain in all Granada. One look at his daughter when she stepped into full womanhood, and in his eyes she changed instantly from child to commodity. The Thousand Doors were those he set between her and the influence of a pernicious outside world that might teach a placid woman the corrupting lessons of decision, disobedience, and independent thought, to say nothing of what she might do without consulting him if once made aware of her beauty's power.

It was his experience that women did not handle such knowledge in a way comfortable for men.

In the days before Granada fell to the Catholic Kings, he immersed himself in unrelenting calculations as to how he might open some few of those thousand doors a crack, purchasing his continued well-being with his daughter's personal coin. Would he haggle out a better deal by bartering his child to the retreating court of Boabdil or to the victorious Christians? Unless Allah hearkened to the prayers of His most faithful servant and miraculously granted the girl two maidenheads, her father must decide. He became so rapt in this project that he overlooked one small, dark fact: the slave of his house and bed named simply *la Zagala*, The wench.

"Well, and does a gypsy need more name than that?"

as *la Zagala* herself has said to me. If she ever had another name, she does not recall it or chooses to conceal it. In this she is in some company, for to this day not one of us—*la Zagala* and the lady Rasha included—have been able to discover the given name of our most mysterious fellow traveler, the little Jewess.

Her tale remains untold, untellable; the lady Rasha's must suffice. I spoke of *la Zagala* the household slave, the master's unpaid whore. Ah, but she was more than that. She was also sole companion to his daughter. He saw no harm in it, being blind.

Where and how they came by the book, neither one will say. The lady Rasha insists it was the gypsy brought it to her attention, claiming that she could not read it but that the pictures were very pretty. *La Zagala* counters with the thorny question of how an impoverished slave such as herself could have obtained so rare and esoteric a volume.

I refrain from suggesting theft. *La Zagala* is no one's slave now, and she is touchy.

Whencever, however the book appeared, it did not long lie idle. The pictures therein were not merely pretty, they were inspirational; the text more so. Preparations were made (some difficult), ceremonies were conducted (some untidy), and words were spoken (all blasphemous). The result was Zamiz.

The lady Rasha says, "No one was more surprised than I to see the success of our modest dabblings. No one, I swear, unless it was my lord Zamiz himself. He stood within the web of dried pigeons' blood and garlic juice which *la Zagala* had traced on the floor of my chamber and demanded to speak with the summoning wizard whose bidding he must now perform." She dimples sweetly as she adds, "Ah, Sister Ana, even your pen could not adequately describe his expression when he learned that the all-mighty sorcerer was two women."

I ask whether anger outweighed puzzlement in that expression, or the other way around.

She answers: "There is a banquet. At the banquet is a golden dish. In the golden dish is a mound of the snowiest, the finest, the most toothsome *khus-khus* mortal man ever tasted. One grain of it upon the tongue is sufficient to convince the most hardened doubter that he has passed away to the True Paradise. Fair maidens stand above the dish and sprinkle it betimes with wafers of beaten gold and droplets of rosewater."

"And?" I think it fair to prod her to the point.

Her dimples deepen. "And in the middle of the *khus-khus* you behold a muddy toad. *That* is how my lord Zamiz the Unaccountably Repulsive first looked at me."

But not for long.

The lady Rasha does not choose to make me privy to the negotiations by which she came to be the demon's bride and he, as dower-gift, imparted to both her and the faithful *la Zagala* so great a measure of magic. I have my assumptions, all based on the hard realities of beauty as coin. Zamiz, too, bargained with more than mere sorcery to lure the lady in. Why else is he termed the *Un*accountably Repulsive?

I have seen enough fair females within my father's domain happily wed to men whose most attractive physical characteristics—let us be charitable—needs must be something their wives alone can see. What this may be, I know not. (Once, as a child, I asked my mother about this. She blushed prettily and said, "It is charm, and God's will." It is not.)

The lady Rasha will no more enlighten me than my mother as to her husband's occult attractions. Nor does she see fit to clarify for me other questions anent our voyage, beyond its goal, such as why our ship sailed through the skies only so far and no farther before descending by gentle degrees to the bosom of the waves.

She shrugs. "It is the will of Allah. Besides, my lord Zamiz has told me that I need not worry my pretty head over details. The ship was his gift to me upon our wedding morn. Then too did he explain to me the great labor at hand, and the urgency thereof." Her eyes sought the West. "The call has been sounded, the faithful turn."

"What call?" I wish to know, and likewise, "Which faithful? For we are as rag-a-bag a sampling of beliefs as ever you could find upon a single keel, my lady."

The lady Rasha's smile is *almost* as condescending as my father's. "Faith and belief and religion are all one to you, are they not, Sister Ana? When you have learned the difference, perhaps you will be able to understand the full nature of our mission. The Genoese professes the same religion as you, yet lodges stronger belief in his ambitions than in any sip of wine or nibble of wafer. As for his faith—" Her sigh is like the dying flutter of a dove.

I accuse her of twisting riddles more convoluted than her people's whole snake-and-grapevine alphabet. Again I receive that smile. I have resolved that if she pats me on the head as she would a gaze-hound, I shall remind her that our patron Santiago is also called *Moor-smiter*. Remind her by example, though her unaccountably repulsive lord makes me smart for it after.

"Sister Ana, shall I trust you in this?" she asks. We are standing by the rail at the violet hour of twilight, I with my fingers wrapped around one of my gull-quill pens, she with her husband's sweetmeat jar cradled against her bosom. The robes she now wears are gossamer, with no more substance to them than a lover's promises. The weather on these seas is far warmer than Palos. I play delicious, daring games with all my mind's conjectures, wondering what Mother Catalina would do were I to appear before her garbed in one of the lady Rasha's cast-offs, my skin a pearly shimmer glimpsed through veils?

"Trust me?" I echo. "That is up to you. But do recall that your lord Zamiz has personally expressed the wish that none interfere with the scribe: myself. My faith—my *religion*, if you prefer—ranks sins of omission as equally heinous with sins of commission. To neglect is to abuse. Tell me as much or as little as you like. I swear it shall go no further than this." I rattle my latest sheet of clean parchment.

"Very well." The lady Rasha fixes her gaze ahead, to where our vessel's bow cleaves the waves.

And so it is that she comes to tell me of a summons that blared forth from the heart of a distant kingdom, a sunset land of ultramar; of a call that blazed as bright as any fiery star across the ebon table of the night. Wizards beheld its nativity and trembled. Creatures of darkness and of dreams crept from their last sanctuaries—the crevices of forgotten houses, the rachitic spines of old books, the hearts of those too humble to assert that all knowledge is mewed up solely between the iron walls of reason—and hearkened to their lord's desire.

He summoned them: He, the one left to reign over a land where things we name monstrous, mythic, evil, all dwell in as much harmony as exists between plain Christian men. Word had reached him, a warning. The last great wall was breached, the thievery of Time had stolen his tranquillity. Brought to him on leathern wings, in the weary beak of a Sierra Nevada-hatched dragonet, came tidings that men were turning their eyes to the setting sun.

And what burned in those eyes? Not the child's gape-mouthed delight in wonders for the sake of wonders. Not hopes of discovering an answer to ills of body or soul. Not even the tattered scholar's homely passion to inch back the greater shadows with each rushdip of knowledge kindled in his mind. None of that. Nothing but greed.

He was not happy. The old agreement had been broken, or at least so warped and riddled with the mouse-nips of passing ages that this wicked—*seepage*, the lady Rasha terms it—could come to pass. He could hardly believe it. His anguish, his uncertainty rolled out in waves that every enchantment-touched being on earth would feel, soon or late. Spells stuttered. Healings went awry. The nightshade blossomed at midday and the phoenix forgot her natal ashes. If the news were true, there was nothing he could do to defer, delay, or deflect what would come.

"So he called out into the far realms, where his more venturesome subjects lingered. If what he heard were true, their homeland was in peril. Something must be decided, something must be done. That is what my lord Zamiz told me. That is why we have undertaken this voyage."

"Yes," I say, though what am I agreeing with? "It is commendable that good vassals respond so readily to their lord's summons, if only to confirm bad news. That much I understand. But—tell me, my lady, why you and your handmaiden have gone to such trouble to secure the presence of the little Jewess among our company. Does she also owe Prester John allegiance? Is she, too, a creature of darkness, a sorceress of great power?"

"Is that what you suspect?" The lady Rasha sounds amused. This rankles.

"Well, I have heard less believable things of the Jews." I am very much on my dignity.

"I do not doubt it." She smiles no more. Her face is as cold and unreadable as the silvered mirror of the moon. "Were she what you think, what need for us to rescue her from the fire? The child is less than your imagination paints her, and more than you can know. We *must* bring her into his court, and soon. Every ill is born twinned to remedy, if Allah but grant us the grace to see it. She may yet be the saving of all that now waits imperiled. So swears my lord Zamiz. Without her, we had as well stayed where we were."

The lady Rasha speaks so passionately that I am confounded. All this, for the transport of one little Jewess? I must protest: "Why is *she* so necessary? The powers of Prester John are legendary. His wealth is vast, yet still outshone by the wonders over which he rules—thus the tales, at any rate. If these be true, what has he to fear from the Genoese and his bobble of boats? A breath of Prester John's command, and your husband might smash their vessels to splinters. Everyone says the western sea teems with monsters. They are expecting the worst. Give it to them."

This time she does not even regard me with the pity bestowed on witlings. "Prester John is your name for him, and so you confuse his ways with those of your own priests." She turns from the rail and from me. I am dismissed without a word, left to scribble down all I can remember of our conversation.

The last thing I hear her say as she returns to her cabin is, "It functions as he promised; I am content."

Would I were similarly at peace.

Nine

The night above me balances on starpoint between midnight and dawn, and here I sit, writing by the moon. How can I sleep now? Ice consumes me from the marrow of my bones outward. If I sleep again, I shall know myself blessed.

Less than two hours past, it happened. As we slept, the air was rent by shrieks so hideous as to congeal the blood in our veins. I sat bolt upright at the first, thinking it an evil dream, but a second scream clawed after the tattered winding-sheet of the first, and a third arose from the grave of night to clutch at those that went before.

"Mercy of God, what is it?" Mother Catalina cried. We were all consigned to a single cabin, through no knowing malice on the lady Rasha's part. She assumes that nuns prefer to huddle together at all times, like sheep.

Sister Angustias had her pearly rosary in her hands and was praying loudly, as if God were hard of hearing. She paused for breath long enough to say, "It is the Devil's work, most certainly." Another *Ave* rattled through, and then: "Send Sister Ana to see."

I set my face against that suggestion; in vain. My late favor with Zamiz might command some respect among the ladies by daylight, but night lent them other faces. A night like this was no exception, when such howls of unadulterated terror tore the velvet silence that they would chance offending the demon's scribe sooner than risk their own necks.

As Sister Angustias herself whispered in my ear, "If you do not go, we shall see whether a bastard floats. Nor shall your ungodly familiars succor you. I have read that not even the most powerful fiend in Hell can bear the touch of the sea."

So I went, for the sake of Christ's sweet charity. I had no time to don my full habit, but left the cabin only in my undergarment of coarse linen. I went with a small oil lamp, its flame sheathed with horn, and my own prayers.

My feet were bare, as always. For fear of being called a fanciful woman I hesitate to record that the gilded rungs of the ladder by which I ascended to the main deck and the beaten brass flooring beneath my soles felt somehow different than the same metals by daylight. Through the callused skin of heel and ball, I could not escape the strangeness of that sensation.

I cannot lie, not even to save myself from whatever cynicism or scorn my diabolic reader may mete out to my portion on scanning these words: It *did* feel different. Not a mere matter of comparative temperature either, explicable as a natural phenomenon, no. Something more potent than rational circumstance infused the very fiber of the ship by moonlight. I cannot explain, nor must I. I can only say that the vessel supped enchantment from a sky of jet and diamond, and passed on no more than a tenuous, ghostly kiss of that great magic to me.

Ah, no, not magic. Though we sail into the very womb of wonders, I am bound to deny enchantment any sovereignty. I must not turn my thoughts so perilously far from the truths I have been drilled to recognize: I am a nun. I am a bride of Christ. There is no magic. God's hand is in all things, His word forbids us all commerce with sorcery.

Yet the night was beautiful, and surely I may see God's hand in that?

And then the screams came again, like some timely reminder of the hellish fate awaiting those who cannot make their hearts subordinate. Alone on the brassy deck, I heard them. They came from the hatchway aft of our own—for the brazen ship had two compartments below-decks. I had always assumed that while the lady Rasha relegated the *Descalzas* and Brother Garcilaso to the forward hold, she reserved the other for whatever goods or ballast her devil-ship carried.

Holding my lamp high, I stepped cautiously nearer the hatchway. The hatch itself was laid to one side on the deck. I knelt beside it, gathering up the long hem of my chemise so as not to tangle myself and pitch into the hold. I know my luck, which waits for me around every corner with an upraised bladder full of pig's blood.

A second soft glow of lamplight mirrored mine from down below. I saw a thick bed of straw, partly overspread with a delicate purple weaving, gold-shot. *La Zagala* hunkered down to one side, tiered skirts kilted high. She looked out of temper. On the other side of the improvised divan a white horse of the divine race of Arabic steeds regarded the black wench with a coolly curious eye.

On the bedding between them lay the little Jewess, her *sanbenito* a crumple of castoff yellow cloth at her feet. She was naked as her mother bore her, her skin pale as new milk, her black hair painted to her flesh with stripes of sweat, her breasts small and round as any young maiden's.

Her belly otherwise.

I must have gasped louder than wisdom should have allowed. *La Zagala*'s head jerked up suddenly, her dark eyes snapped onto mine like manacles. "Well, will you turn out to be a black-robed booby like the rest, or useful? Come down! We are in a bad way here."

"What—what is wrong with her?" Thus I stammered, and thus *la Zagala* came to skew her mouth up into the quizzical twist most folk reserve for viewing harmless idiots.

"Just come down," she said. She sounded too weary to lance my shortcomings with her tongue.

I did as she bid me, taking great care not to foul my feet in the hem of my undergarment. Waiting for no further direction from the black wench, I took my place opposite her across the little Jewess' swollen belly. My lamp I set as far from the horse's hooves and the poor, suffering girl's thrashings as I might. Brass does not burn, but straw can work a mischief. I could see we needed no additional troubles.

La Zagala mopped the little Jewess' brow with a folded square of leek-green cloth, then swept sweat from her own with the back of her hand. "Too soon," she said with a sigh. "Too damned soon, and now who'll be the better for all we've gone through?" She addressed her remarks solely to the little Jewess' belly. I swear, her intentness led me to believe it might reply!

Then she lifted that small, keen chin of hers at me and demanded, "What do you know about birth, virgin?"

It was my turn to silently let her know I thought her mad. This, but for a moment. Truth must shatter every wall of image and illusion we set between it and the world. I am a virgin, true, but innocence need not claim ignorance for fear of being doubted.

"I have seen two women give birth," I told the gypsy. "My mother sometimes went to help the midwife." The little Jewess uttered another of those horrific howls. Her belly stiffened, blue veins stark against the cream of her skin, then seemed to ripple like the sea. She gasped, poor child, and her hands groped to clutch at something more than cloth and straw.

My hand slipped beneath her searching fingers. She gripped it tightly, with a strength of sinew and bone that left both her knuckles and my own white. I saw no more than a sliver of color beneath her lashes. Then the wrenching of her belly subsided and her eyelids closed, though I know she did not sleep. I laid my other hand atop hers and said, "There, my dear, don't worry. I think I can recall a trick or two they used to make births come easier."

Yes, this to a Jewess. And I tell it so that none may mistake it for the folly of a moment: *I would do it all again.* There. Four strokes of the quill to underline my iniquity. I would grant all comfort and aid in my power to the child even if an angel of the Lord appeared to me at that very moment, the thorny crown and the bloody spear and the nails themselves in his hands.

But if I burn for this, then tell me whether He lied who vowed mercy to the merciful.

"She can't hear you," *la Zagala* informed me. She refolded the green cloth to expose a part of it not yet soaked through with sweat. "I think she's dropped off into a doze. All to the good. The shock of hearing kindness from one of you lot might kill her." Her words were flint, but the flicker of a smile softened them. "You are not much like your sisters." This came as purest compliment, and may God forgive me, I accepted it in the same spirit.

Gently I disengaged my hand from that of the little Jewess. "Is there more I can do here before she wakes? Shall I fetch water?"

The wench laughed, and the white steed nudged me with his velvet muzzle. The soft pressure of that urging made me turn and see a small keg, its staves gold hooped with silver, brimful of water so fresh and sweet its scent alone conjured visions of mountain streams. The horse whickered. Holy Mary my witness, there was knowledge in the beast's golden eye, and a spark that would have been called good humor if kindled beneath human brows.

"Don't tell me *you* fetched that, friend!" I exclaimed, making a jest of it as I stroked his satiny nose.

But there was no jest to be made. "He did," *la Zagala* remarked as if this were the way of the world and I a mooncalf for wondering at it. "From the mainland, however distant that may be. He won't say. He has his uses, but he is too whimsical and stubborn to be of real help. We must take what he offers and not hope for more."

Seeing me agape, she added, "Oh, this skin he wears now is just for convenience's sake; his, no one else's." To the horse she said, "Show yourself as you are."

Nothing happened. The steed merely cocked his head and flared his nostrils.

La Zagala snapped her fingers. "I told you he's stubborn. He'll change when he's got a mind to. If he hasn't let the knowledge dribble out his ears. His kind can't handle two thoughts at once without breaking one and getting the other backwards."

"Oh, can't we?" said the horse, and the snowy coat melted into a flood of scales the color of fine aquamarines. Thinly webbed fingers fell upon my shoulders, making me shudder with surprise at their warmth where they touched bare skin. His breath stirred a hot prickling in my ear. I jerked my head around to avoid that disturbing feeling and my lips brushed the feathery growths bearding his face. His grin was sharp, short, and the white of sun-bleached bone.

"You speak?" Truth forces me to write out the evidence of how foolishly I questioned him. "How do you come to know Castilian? Is this—your master's work?" For a mage as great as Prester John may certainly bestow the gift of speech where it pleases him.

The merman drew back his head with serpentine ease and from that little distance looked me over thoroughly. He seemed to be taking my measure, somehow. He would not reply.

La Zagala grunted. "He doesn't understand why you

are so surprised to hear him speak. All this is as natural to him as breath. Underwater folk have no use for words, so mind touches mind. I may not understand how that can be, but I'm told that's how it is. Up here with us, he can wriggle into your thoughts just as easily as an eel slips into a jug and help himself to whatever he finds: Castilian, French, Arabic, Greek, all as one to him.''

Well, that made some sense. And what a fool I was to be more daunted when the merman spoke than when he slipped out of his horse-skin! Sister Angustias might have accepted his gift of tongues without a blink—the God of her heaven speaks purest Castilian exclusively, but Satan is a linguist—yet she would have screamed for Brother Garcilaso and all the Cardinals of Rome if the merman shifted shape before her. We each of us have our own distinct tolerance for the nature of the miracles we can swallow whole.

I bowed my head to the merman. "My thanks, good sir, for any help you can give us now with this poor child." I picked up the rumpled *sanbenito* from the foot of the pallet and shook it out, then laid it gently over the little Jewess while she drowsed.

"Help?" He squatted most immodestly, so that I had to avert my eyes. "I brought sweet water. I was told to do it, and I did. I was told to stay until *she* says I can go." He fanned one paw at *la Zagala*. "But I won't go, if this one hatches." A second gesture indicted the little Jewess. "I will be the first to see him, then. I will have many fish, and possibly the young turtles, before I will tell the others how he was born to us."

"You will leave when you're told, Greedygut," *la*

Zagala informed him. "And if we have the ill luck to see him born before this ship touches land, you won't make a profit from it. I'll see to that. He comes for all your kind, not just the few who'd like it otherwise. Your say-so won't keep anyone from sharing in his birth."

"Where he's born, it's blessed." The merman put out a green tongue covered with tiny, raspy white hooks. "Even I know it. If he's born at sea, he's ours."

"A curse is yours: May your webbing wither!" the gypsy shouted. The merman quailed, balling himself up behind me, as if curses, like arrows, must stop at the first barrier they meet.

I did not make any objection to being used as a wall. I was too stunned by what I heard. My father's pet belief is that a woman, like a horse, must be led blinkered from a burning stable, for she is incapable of connecting the fact of fire with the implication of personal harm. But I can thread together more than beads.

"Friend," I said to *la Zagala*, mastering the tremor from my voice. "You speak of a blessed birth here. Then am I to assume—?"

The gypsy's teeth blinded me silent. "If you know the mark of virginity, I'll give you leave to look for it. *Discreetly.* Wake her and I'll thump you on the head so you'll remember me. Or you could take my word for it."

I rested my eyes on the little Jewess. "Virgin. . . ." The word held a new world, as did the presence dreaming within the curve of her womb. I began to pray.

Ten

. We kept watch beside her, *la Zagala* and the merman and I. I think it must have been the better part of an hour. The merman became bored and left before less than half that time passed. I heard the muffled splash as he returned to his true element. When he was gone, the only sounds within that hold were my whispered orisons, and the ghost of sea-swell heard through brazen walls, and the little Jewess' sleeping breaths. *La Zagala* did not seem to need to breathe. Arms on knees she sat, her dark eyes like embers.

At last she said, "You might as well go. It's passed. A false start, nothing more; I've seen many such. Our luck might yet hold and we'll get her ashore before the child comes. If not—" Another shrug.

"But why is it so important that he be born ashore?" I asked.

No clue of meaning surfaced on her impassable expression. "What's that to you, little holy·crow? You're tucked up safe in salvation's pouch already. Go back to your kin and share their satisfaction in knowing that all the rest of creation's bound for hell but you. Snug and smug, you are, and liking it.'' She turned her shoulder to me and readjusted the covering on the little Jewess.

I tried to object, but realized that I had not the faintest idea of where to begin refuting her arguments. Instead I changed tack and topic both, asking, ''Do you think it will be soon, then, that we encounter land?''

La Zagala did not think it important to meet my eyes. ''Who knows?'' she told the little Jewess' belly. ''The merfolk don't wander too far from landfall, but there may be scattered isles in these waters that extend their range. It's the mainland we seek, the high court, the Gryphon Palace by the Dragon Road.''

I clapped my hands into my armpits and shivered. Was it from the cold? My shift was thin, but the hold was no cooler than when I'd first descended. ''The Gryphon Palace, the Dragon Road—How do you know so much of a place you've never seen?''

''The same way you know of Heaven,'' the black wench countered. ''By placing more or less faith in what I've read and what others tell me. It may be I am wrong . . . or that you are.'' Her sharp chin dipped over the little Jewess. ''*She* has some luck foreseeing things—take that as a sign of what you will—but she hasn't made a pronouncement in days. I'm no sadder for it. She always predicted gloom.''

Given the likely prospects of her people, I could see why the little Jewess specialized in doomsayings. Grief was the circumstance with which she was most experienced. Of this I said nothing to *la Zagala*, but instead, ''Good night.''

I took up my horned lamp and climbed out of the hold. As I padded from that hatchway to my own, I wondered how I was going to explain the source of the screams to my waiting sisters.

Now I realize it is of little consequence. I have other things to think of, much yet to write as the night wanes. My sisters will not care how late I return to them or even if I ever do. Into their laps I will drop some slight plausibility or other to explain the earlier commotion they heard; that is, if they have not already gone back to sleep by this.

And what fills their dreams? I do not know, nor can I guess whether Mother Catalina's strict rule permits us any dreams at all. This night I have seen much, yet willingly would I lose all that I have learned if it would purchase me the certainty that the last thing I saw was but a dream.

It was not.

I spied him just as I emerged from the hatchway. He is the only man aboard who does not slap flippered feet across a metal deck, nor spend his idle hours curled up among candied apricots. I marked his shape, his gait, and the flash of moonshine from his tonsured head just as he dodged around one corner of the poop cabin.

Brother Garcilaso was no dream, none of night's fictions.

So here I sit, by starlight, writing all that has passed as if the flow of ink onto paper has the leeching power to drain dread from my blood. My little light guttered out a while since. I have cudgeled memory to provide every detail of this night's doing as a distraction for my troubled soul. Still, the truth will not be cocooned, its edges to be glimpsed blunt through the spidersilk of other events. In the end I must face what I cannot soften or deny.

Brother Garcilaso knows. He had come up on deck for whatever reason, in an accursed hour. He had heard much from the open hatchway where the little Jewess lay, drawn nearer, seen, heard more. Then, like a weasel with an egg in its mouth, he ran off with the precious secret.

What will he do with it?

My lord Zamiz, as you value this strange cargo your ship bears, tell me what Brother Garcilaso will do.

Eleven

Land.

Twelve

Peace at last, and not a day too soon. The palanquin sways abominably. The lady Rasha tells me that such conveyances were originally intended for camelback. To strap one such atop a gryphon's spine is asking for discomfort. The beast resents it, and the wings get in the way. Too, when a gryphon is annoyed, it tends to exude a certain—*musk*, the lady Rasha calls it, and holds a spiceball to her nose. I call it *stink*, name it thus plainly, and try to lean well clear of the palanquin when I vomit from the fumes.

We have been on the road three days: The Dragon Road, no less, though the dragons are not the only ones who inhabit these parts. Yes, three days since we made landfall, and another day before that when we were still asea, and not a word of answer from Zamiz; not one. A curse on him!

This I can safely write, without fear of criticism. He has gone, my patron; Zamiz rides with us no more. The moment that the lady Rasha's hennaed foot touched land, the earthenware jar in her hands spontaneously burst to red dust, leaving her fingers dripping golden fruit and syrup. Deaf to her curses as he proved blind to my written pleas, Zamiz the Unaccountably Repulsive whirled up from our midst in the form of a black wind and flew away to the northwest. His exultant laughter darkened the sky. The small delegation from Prester John's court come to welcome us ashore all shook and fell to their knees at the demon's passing. I did not know that gryphons had knees until this.

Brother Garcilaso soiled himself. Maybe Sister Angustias too, though in these robes of ours, who can tell?

At first we were offered regal steeds for our individual use. Mother Catalina forbade it, thin-lipped and utterly disapproving of the mounts offered us. So sad to waste such magnificent coursers! And could they help it if they had been born with the upper parts of men? I saw the disappointment in their eyes, poor souls, but Mother Catalina was adamant. So we were to walk.

The path from the sea was easy going, smooth as buttermilk until it broadened out to join the fabled Dragon Road. Your dragon is an acquisitive worm, but nowhere famed for neatness. To either hand we beheld the pinched-up, wrinkled flanks of gray-green mountains, all pocked with the great serpents' lairs. From every cavern maw where the tenant was absent there poured a cascade of gems and gold, many tumbling down to clutter the roadway. At least in those caves where the worm was at home, his dozing bulk and grasping talons held the precious hoard secure beneath him, like glittering, faceted bedclothes.

Have you ever walked barefoot over jewels? The clumsier jumble of gold chains and bracelets are likewise rough terrain. Not even Brother Garcilaso and all my sisters working together were able to gather up enough of the scattered treasure to clear the path entirely. There was always more gold, more jewels, and the occasional pile of bright yellow dragon's dung to mock their efforts and hinder our passage. If this were not enough, my fellow Christians were so hampered with all the riches they had tucked and stowed and tied up in every utile inch of their clothing that it took only the smallest misstep to send them sprawling.

Sister Angustias began to complain. She enumerated her ancestors, the better to make our hosts realize the magnitude of her person. None of Prester John's servants paid her any mind. When she tried to bind her gleanings to the back of one of the horse-men, he lashed out with his hooves and came near to granting her an unexpectedly early reunion with her Bridegroom.

That was when Mother Catalina told me I was to carry Sister Angustias' haul of treasure. "You are too proud, Sister Ana." My sins whined shrilly through her nose. "While we all labor to accept this bounty that Our Lord has set before us—which sacred gift shall be placed wholly in the service of our poor convent when we return—you do nothing. Rather than see you condemn yourself to eternal flame, I will show you the proper path." And she did. The weight of all Sister Angustias' gathered gold combined with the gems Mother Catalina herself had gathered bent my back so that I could look nowhere but the path beneath my feet.

The first night, our train stopped beneath the shelter of

one of the larger mountain caverns. The master of the place came forth to greet us. He looked to be an ancient, though his limbs were straight beneath the rainbowed robe he wore and his eyes were clear. Long, silver whiskers trailed from his chin, a beard like a comet's frosty tail. A mottled serpent, scarlet and green with golden eyes, wreathed his shoulders. He spoke a word, and it spread purple wings, flittering away into the depths of the cavern beyond. The unburdened gryphons of our cavalcade followed it.

That night I ate strange food and drank strange wine. Creatures like men a handspan high scrambled here and there at the old man's bidding, ordering rich cloths over tables that seemed to have burgeoned into our world from the realm of living stone. Faces green and narrow as willow leaves flitted shy glances at me from split-pupiled eyes. Brother Garcilaso and my sisters shrank themselves down at one end of the board, but I sat where I might have an ear in either camp, as it were. Much good it did me. The tongue our escorts used was all trills, ripples, barks, and incomprehensibilities.

We were conducted to a room where silk-covered piles of down lined great cups of stone; our beds. I crept into mine cautiously, seizing the edge in panic when the whole affair began to teeter. A portion of the stone broke away in my hand. I ran my fingers along the chalky edge of the eggshell, thicker than a child's thigh, and wondered what sort of being had fledged from that first nest. I was too weary to wonder long, and slept well.

We left at dawn. I was roused before this by two of Prester John's servants. One looked like an ordinary man, though he was not too modestly dressed. A flurry of saffron pleats slashed from his right shoulder to just above the knee. Laughing-faced bands of gold and topaz bound his upper arms, and a duke's prison-price of canary diamonds webbed in gold covered his dark hair. His companion did not affect so much luxury, a ruby nose-stud being enough for him. As his face protruded from his chest, this was still most effective ornamentation.

"The princess Zamiz requires you ride today," he rumbled. His companion, who could, inclined his head in confirmation.

I entered the palanquin and was greeted by the lady Rasha—in this land called the princess Zamiz. From her comfort among the cushions she held out to me a bundle of broad, pale brown leaves and a fan of new-cut quills. Within the fairly spacious precincts of the palanquin was a place for me opposite hers, and a shelf cunningly built into one corner, where a silver-capped inkhorn awaited.

"But what am I to do with these when I finish?" I protested, waving the crinkled sheets before her. I did not think it prudent to mention her husband's precipitate departure.

The lady Rasha was wise enough to infer my true meaning. "Until such time as my lord Zamiz may conveniently return, you are still his chosen scribe. I myself shall see to providing you with the necessities of your craft, and the safe disposal of those pages you complete. It would be an unfortunate occurrence should my lord return, and demand to see what chronicles you had kept in his absence, and learn that his wishes in this matter had not been followed."

In this, I agreed. I then attempted to tell her of my fears, kindled that last night but one aboard ship.

"And has your Brother Garcilaso said anything to you about the little Jewess, or her child?" the lady Rasha asked.

"Nothing," I admitted.

The corner shelf on her side of the palanquin held a bowl of sweetmeats, a thoughtful attention of our escorts. The lady Rasha might miss her husband, but not his attendant tidbits. Idly she picked through these and told me, "Then we have no worries. Perhaps he did not hear or see so much as you fear. Perhaps he knows nothing at all."

"God grant it," I replied. Then the whole palanquin lurched as the gryphon set out, and I was soon busily scribbling away to recapture all that had passed since Zamiz flew off. God grant my humble memory has been faithful to the truth, for I feel I have acquitted myself of my duty to the best of my ability.

I wish I had more to write. It keeps me from being sick quite so violently as when I—

Thirteen

"Speak, child. Do not be afraid of it."

"But I am afraid, lord."

"Of what? Of the contrivance?"

"Of you."

"You must speak louder than that. I have heard mice more thunderous. Am I so terrible to look upon, then?"

"No."

"What? You must speak up, I tell you. The contrivance cannot always—"

"*No.*"

"Ah. Better. Then if I am not such a horror, why fear me?"

"Because you are Prester John."

"As much as you are Sister Ana. And you, at least, have some legitimate claim to your ecclesiastical title. Mine, I fear, would not survive the close scrutiny of your churchly companions."

"Then what are you, lord? Are you—a wizard?"

"Would you name yourself so?"

"You are laughing at me, lord."

"I am *smiling* at you, my child, as I might fondly smile at any of my treasured friends."

"Am I then your—friend?"

"Oh, more! Much more than that! My benefactress, to whom I stand indebted for much useful knowledge and many a weary evening's hour beguiled. Come! Have I startled you?"

"Lord, until a truly short while ago, I had never laid eyes on you. The instant we arrived at the palace steps, two of your attendants appeared and told me I must go with them. They brought me here, into your presence—"

"—and you did not know who I was, at first. I will never forget the way your little mouth curled in perplexity. I could almost hear you wondering: *Who is this fat old Nubian? What is he doing here?*"

"Lord, I never—!"

"But yes, you did. And so you will admit, if you are so great an acolyte of the truth as you declare. Well, I *am* fat. See, even through these loose cotton robes you cannot help but observe how my flesh jiggles. Nor can you deny its hue. *I am black, but comely, O ye daughters of Jerusalem, as the tents of Kedar, as the curtains of Solomon.* Well, perhaps I am not all that comely."

"Lord, it pleases you to jest with me. How can you claim me for your benefactress?"

"Then these—Ha! Catch that one! It's fluttered from the pile, and the balcony is open. I wouldn't want to lose a single leaf—these are not yours?"

"My manuscript!"

"Ah, you were not half so ecstatic to see me. But I am an old man, and disappointment was my milk-brother."

"Oh, no, lord! You mustn't think—It's only that I never expected to see these pages again. How—?"

"From the hand of Zamiz to my own. I have my small arts. And I am eagerly waiting to review whatever further lines you may have penned on the overland journey. Your style, my dear, is utterly refreshing. You embroider nothing, but stitch a fine, clear seam of pure observation. I am tired of the Irish bards, but the fairy women can never seem to get enough of them. Not a day goes by but they've lured another one westward. Would they but choose paramours with more legible handwriting and fewer overwrought banalities. Tir na n'Oc, indeed!"

"Lord, I don't understand."

"You needn't. I have not summoned you to improve your understanding, but to make you a gift."

"What? That—thing?"

"I call it my contrivance, but *thing* does very well. Yes, I wish to make your task easier. See how small it is! It can fit in the palm of your hand. Take it, carry it wherever you like in my realm, and it will record all you hear, every word you speak to it."

"Incredible."

"No. Listen."

. . .

"Oh! My lord!"

"Clever, isn't it? You need never again fear the loss of a single word, nor depend solely on your memory."

"You mean—I am still to be—to write—?"

"Still the scribe, yes. Still *my* scribe, my chronicler, my witness where others would sooner forget or gloss away what happens. For great things shall happen, child. Wonders hover above these shores.''

"But—but, lord, what need has one with your powers of me? With this device—''

"So now it is elevated to *device* from *thing*. What next, I wonder.''

"Lord, please. I only wish to know why you might not carry the—*thing* with you and make your own chronicle.''

"Because, dear one, I am Prester John. Have you not heard of me? I rule a vast domain of unguessed riches. The smallest gem I wear upon my smallest finger would be enough to ransom the Pope and all his Cardinals. Half an ell of fabric from my meanest robe would redeem the Holy Land. The lowest villein in my service—''

"But it's cotton.''

"What?''

"Your robe. It's plain cotton, and there's a grease stain on it. Half an ell of that wouldn't redeem a dunghill.''

"That depends on the dunghill, doesn't it? What a pretty smile you have, Sister Ana. And what a keen intelligence. Both are wasted behind convent walls, I fear. Yes, you see through to the heart of many things. Perhaps you can answer your own question. Why do I not merely use this contrivance of mine to make my own chronicles of what shall pass?''

"My lord—''

"Think.''

"I think—I think perhaps it is because you are Prester John. If you walk among Brother Garcilaso and Mother

Catalina and the rest, their faces change. They bow and
flatter, speak and act the way they think you wish to have
them. Your contrivance would soon choke on all their
pretense, and you would only chronicle lies."

"Ah."

"Lord . . . you are crying?"

"Only an old man's way. You have made me very
happy, really. Do not trouble—There. I am better. You
see, then, Sister Ana, why it must be you."

"Yes. To learn what Brother Garcilaso plans against
the baby."

"*If*, my dear; *if* he plans anything at all."

"You should kill him now, and be sure. The baby will
be safe certainly, then. It would be easy: One of your
gryphons might snatch him up and let him fall from a
great height. One of your dragons might tear him to
pieces."

"You might burn him alive in the fires of your eyes,
child. No; we do no killing. We have left that to others.
But still, there is no reason not to remain informed, fore-
warned. Will you do me this continued service?"

"Yes, but—"

"But—?"

"Please, with paper. And ink and quills. Your contrivance is a marvel, but I was not bred to marvels. Sometimes, too, there is so much more to preserve of an
incident besides what words are uttered. I would not
want you to lose anything to half-truths."

"And—?"

"And I don't like the way your contrivance makes my

voice sound: Shrill, like a piglet's squeal; piping as a bat's squeak.''

"Then you shall have your quills and ink again, and your paper. And your gentle vanity preserved. As for this poor, unappreciated contrivance of mine—"

Fourteen

The little Jewess sleeps in a bed carved of coral, rose and pearl. Her bedclothes are airiest gossamer beneath, quilted satin above. Her *sanbenito* is gone, flamed to ash in the single breath of the palace's smallest serving-dragon. Now she is attired in samite, white and gold and heaven blue, with the petals of ten thousand flowers strewn anywhere she chooses to set her naked feet.

She is never alone, nor allowed to feel anything less than fervently desired. Her attendants are beautiful maidens whose skin is milk, whose hair and eyes are emerald, whose swan-wings are silverfrost. All of them ask nothing more than her continued happiness, though their blood be its price. They would immediately perform any duty she might require of them, without question. Failing this, they anticipate her wishes so perfectly that even before she can ask for a thing, it is done. This is all to the good, under the circumstances.

She has gone mute. She has gone quite mad.

I like to write by her bedside. No one disturbs me here. No one comes unasked, unless it be Prester John himself and his suite. She does not ask for anyone. It is very quiet in these rooms.

She no longer walks abroad in the Gryphon Palace. The first day we arrived, while I was closeted with Prester John, she was taken from her palanquin and seated on an alabaster throne set with sapphires. Gilded poles banded with the dim fire of opals raised it aloft, each borne by two men whose bull-horned brows were garlanded with eglantine. They carried her through halls of ever-increasing splendor, until they reached the figured bronze doors of these apartments.

Here her attendants burst forth, greeting her with a part-song that hailed the little Jewess by every grandiloquent title one might spin out, given enough idle time and insufficient talent. She was stripped, bathed, anointed, most tenderly examined, and garbed as an empress.

All this she told me that first night, when the banquet was laid to welcome us into Prester John's realms. She was really rather taken with all the attention and desperate to share her joy with someone. I doubt that her chatter was a ploy to maintain this new, alien reality by force of words alone. She is too innocent for such sophisticated sorceries. Children are notorious for accepting extraordinary events as ordinary circumstance. Knowing so little of the world, how can they tell whether it is not in the normal run of things for one to be nigh death one day, nigh worship the next? Youth's resiliency permitted her to adjust.

She was very happy all through dinner. I saw her laughing, clapping her hands while cat-faced birds executed an exotic aerial ballet, their pathways through the air made visible by trails of magically appearing marguerites. The flowery rain turned to real pearls when they drifted down and touched the floor, but further changed to pellets of old cheese when Sister Angustias and the rest tried scooping them into their napkins. Sister Angustias' unfitting language made the little Jewess laugh harder.

Then the banquet ended. The last crumbs were cleared away by clever monkeys, yellow, with eyes like ripe plums. Prester John rose from his place on the dais. He sat alone beneath a crimson canopy made lovely with gold and silver embroideries and a scattering of unobtrusive gems. The massive table before him vanished at a word, the blue marble board falling to dust that made its four golden criosphynx supporters sneeze and stalk off shaking their rams' horns, gravely offended.

He spoke at length, did Prester John, but not anywhere near long enough to give Brother Garcilaso any fear of competition. I will be forgiven, or not, but I do not choose to immortalize his words here. Most speeches of welcome sound the same, and all are equally lacking in sincerity.

However, I must memorialize his deeds, for these did accompany his words to such effect that the most blatant platitudes gained an edge to prick the drowsy listener attentive.

He spoke of the world from which we, his visitors, had come: In his plump hands, a globe of luminous glass formed. In size it was scarcely bigger than a quail's egg; to begin. Quickly it dilated, a solid raindrop into which flowed a stream of its invisible brethren, each adding to the ever-swelling volume of the first until, twice as big as a man's head, it balanced spinning on Prester John's thumb.

He spoke of the lands to which he welcomed us: A second sphere passed from behind the first to take equal pride of place in Prester John's other hand. He spread his arms to their fullest. The twin globes twirled: the first compounded of rippling blues and greens, dappled over with streaks of white like springtime snows; the second all the gaiety of wine and turquoise, amber and malachite sparks. We stared, and the delightful pageantry of captive colors subtly stole their way into solid forms.

In the first globe I saw Palos again, and the shady cloisters of *las Descalzas*. The globe tilted before my eyes, and its dance bore me back to my father's house when joy still dwelled there for me. False joy, but I am not the only one who would dwell with loving lies above harsh truths, given the choice. What choice? We are given none.

In the other orb I saw the full extent of Prester John's domain, a land more beautiful than the Queen of Heaven, a paradise of enchantments to ravish the soul. Dragons glimmered across a flowery lagoon in the purple twilight. Silvery blue grasses parted to the beating of bright wings as jade horses climbed the skies. In mountain hideaways of carnelian cliffs and peridot chasms, great cats with marigold eyes and human breasts suckled infant satyrs.

I could have wept when Prester John next spoke, for his words were like the blaze of noonday sun on the tender morning-glory vine. The globes he held out for our delight withered. I cannot tell which one I mourned for more.

He spoke of how wonderful a world may be that leaves

itself some room for marvels. What man can explain everything he sees? Who is the fool who cannot enjoy unless he dissects a miracle with questions? He is the same who weeps when he learns that some things, once picked apart, can never recover the ember of vitality that made them live. It flies with the first cold incision of the mind, and does not return.

He spoke of this, I think. I cannot be certain. My eyes were too ravished by the new rarities he summoned from thin air. Sphere after sphere, each came sailing through the warm air of the banquet hall at his word. All were fancies of his invention, songs given shape, creations complex and rich in their content.

Here in a single ball were men with limbs of copper, faces hidden by great, towering masks of feathered gold. They mounted a flight of precipitous stone stairs to the throb of giant drums and the shrilling of bone whistles. Black knives winked like glassy stars in their hands, and there was much blood.

In another, a lone man raced through forests deeper and greener than any miserable remnants of trees in all Spain. A stone axe bobbed from his belt, and soft slippers, exquisitely beaded, hushed his passage. He burst into a clearing, and I saw long houses like huge, fallen logs from which a bright-eyed, black-haired people streamed to welcome him.

Splendor filled a third sphere, rooms splashed with gold. Magnificently dressed men passed through, indifferent to the wealth surrounding them. Through an open doorway, I glimpsed a mighty chain of mountains, and birds whose wingspan seemed to enfold the sun.

And there were more. Colors blazed and roistered as each microcosm vied with its neighbor to see which might outdo the rest in the bounty of its prodigies. Birds, beasts, plants, people, even the very insects of the air and the fish of the waters competed in a tournament of beauty. The orbs hung suspended by no thread I could perceive, encircling Prester John's uncrowned head like a wreath of stars.

His assembled subjects applauded the pageant politely—those whom nature had endowed with hands, that is. Melodious chirrings, liquid trills, the slap of webbing and the well-regulated stamping of cloven hooves against mosaic floors coupled with the subdued boom of carefully restrained wings. All these contributed to the atmosphere of bland approval. Their sovereign's arts were commonplace to them.

I stole a glance to either side. My own companions were not taking our host's display half so tranquilly. Mother Catalina was crossing herself at such a rate that she got it wrong a time or two. Sister Angustias' rosary chattered like an old man's teeth. Brother Garcilaso's face was so pinched in disapproval that any further tightening of his mouth or squint of his eyes would cause the whole ugly structure to cave in upon itself. The others—Magdalena, Incarnación, Elena—were as enraptured as I; until they caught sight of Mother Catalina's expression, that is, and trimmed their sails according to that sour breeze.

Then, the final saying: Prester John dismissed his bobbling toys. Obediently they wafted back into invisibility. Four ponderous steps took him down from the dais to the splendid sawn ivory table where the little Jewess sat, princess to his king.

"I will tell all of you a story," he said. These words I recall. It is unthinkable that ever I forget them. *All of you,* he said, but his eyes held fast to hers.

"Now, as once before, men come from the East in search of marvels." He cupped his hands above the little Jewess' head, and glowing water filled them. "Now, as then, they only half-know what they seek and cannot at all guess what they shall find." He released his grasp, and butterflies showered her dark locks as she laughed with pure pleasure.

"Not every surprise is welcome." Prester John's huge shoulders slumped. "To undertake so great a journey, with its attendant perils, and discover that journey's end is not all you expected—Well! Someone must have made you a promise and broken it. To seek a mighty king, enthroned in splendor, and discover a poor woman's infant, wailing among his soiled swaddlings, is a great shock. Someone must repay."

"The East?" I heard Mother Catalina's scandalized hiss. "Brother Garcilaso, he cannot mean—?"

'He cannot." Brother Garcilaso's face was a knotted rope. He had passed judgment; it must therefore be so.

Prester John did no seem to care about what Brother Garcilaso had decided he could not be. He spoke on, without the merest sleight of hand to lighten the words he must say:

"To be cheated of your expectations—If you are a man like most men, you will not tolerate such treatment, believe me! Words are said in haste and bitterness. You refuse to recognize that miracles need not come with fanfare or in surges of light. They do not always roost in palaces. You are a man proud of your knowledge, your distant throne, your riches. You have condescended to attend a promised miracle, and it is unworthy of your own importance. The mother of the brat does not even have the grace to offer you refreshment, and her ancient husband is so toothless you must strain to understand the bastard dialect of Aramaic he speaks. You think perhaps that you will have a word in that other king's ear when you head home again, the Romans' tame king who questioned you so eagerly when you passed through his lands courting the false promise of a star. After all, he is brother royalty. He will laugh at you a little for your gullibility, but he will treat you as befits all that you are."

He took a deep breath so that his jowls shuddered. The little Jewess sat with heavily bejeweled hands flat atop the table, whiter than the ivory they touched. She laughed no more. Her lips too had paled, and her eyes grew like an owl's.

Prester John said on: "The king is pleased to see you and to hear your tale. You share a fine jest at the expense of the others, who fled his realm by a different route. Perhaps they are too ashamed to admit their error; who knows? Later on, while you sleep in a chamber far more appropriate to your station than the dung-fouled straw of a stable, you dream of the jangle of harness and breastplate, the tramp of thickly sandaled feet racing through the darkened streets. It is only a dream.

"You wake to the blood. There are more poor women in this kingdom than you dreamed, yet their grief is as rich and lunatic as that of their betters. In the dead eyes of a throat-slit babe, you see a cold reflection of the evil you have done. You cannot deny a sin whose stench will not be covered over by a mountain of myrrh.

"In the palace, alone with the mocking echo of the great king's laughter, you seek death as the fitting atonement. You try the blade, but its edge splits like the skin of a ripe fig, and suddenly there are too many angels. Very suddenly they have come to you, and rudely, but you know you do not merit courtesy any more than you deserve life. They see it otherwise. Their wrath shatters the sword. The beating of their wings deafens you, and the ugliness within you cringes before their burning beauty, which is pure. Your spirit groans beneath its own inadequacy.

"Their voices are honey sweet, their words are gall. The innocent have paid the price of your greed, your pride. The weak have suffered, the helpless have perished. You will not die. Instead, you will be given keeping of a world where that which is most innocent, most weak, most helpless and most beautiful may take refuge."

He knelt before the little Jewess, grunting with the effort of maneuvering so huge a body to its knees. Hands clasped in prayer, he said, "And because you know greed so well, and pride, and pettiness of soul, you are charged to keep watch against the coming of these unholy three. For the angels warn you that men may take salvation and beat it into the shape of a sword. They may take the humble gift of the stable and raise it to a palace it was never meant to fill. For greed's sake, and power's sake, and simply because they have the might to enforce their desires, they will build a wall around the peace that might have been and deck it with shields and bones."

"And fire." These were the first words I heard the little Jewess utter. Her flesh had turned to snow.

"You see!" Prester John was transformed by happiness. His hands fell hungrily on hers, as if he and she were lovers. "And seeing, you must know that those three ships now sailing west carry men who will despoil at their pleasure, certain that their every whim breathes righteousness. It is not robbery, when those from whom you steal are damned. It is not murder, when you deny those you slay the possibility of a soul."

"A soul?" The little Jewess' voice was a whisper. Her eyes slowly traveled the compass of extraordinary beings filling Prester John's great hall. I read the unspoken question of her heart: *Can such as these have souls?* My gaze trailed after hers, and in the silence of my own mind another question formed: *Who are we, to claim we know the only name of God?*

"A soul." Prester John spoke firmly. "A soul and salvation for it. Salvation and a savior to bring it, so that when those three ships do finally make land, my subjects may meet them as equals in the sight of Him whose hand alike made man and manticore, djinni and Genoese." Reverently he steepled his hands over the gentle swelling of her robes. "And all this, through you."

The little Jewess lowered her head. The mound of her belly was all that she could see. "A savior. . . ." The word trailed away into the silence that was to close over her from that moment on.

Prester John talked to her—at her—for several minutes

longer before he realized that something was amiss. A
man such as himself, inured to the miraculous, could
have no idea of the burden he had asked—commanded
her to accept, with so little preamble.

Did sweet Mary fare any better when she received her
own measure of grace? I wonder. But then, the message
came to her in an angel's mouth. Angels have the power
to heal instantly any harm of spirit or mind that their
unasked-for tidings bring.

Prester John was king and mage; no angel. At last he
saw what he had done, but lacked the power to undo it.
The little Jewess was conducted from the banquet hall by
her airy servants. Prester John pulled himself to his feet
and faced his congregation sheepishly.

"All will be well," he said. His words shook as badly as
the slack flesh of his arms; there was no certainty in that
saying. "Once the child is born, all will be well, I promise
you." He managed to smile.

They cheered him. Was this faith, or merely hope?
Belief given voice, or a noisy, fearful warding off of
doubt? I cannot guess. All that has been asked of me is
that I write, and so I do. I write, and sit here at the little
Jewess' bedside where it is so peaceful, waiting.

And I dread. Yes—may God forgive a woman's heart
that fears a cradle emptied of all but shadows—this, too,
I do.

Fifteen

"Ah! You startled me, Sister Ana."

"Mother Catalina has always taught us that it is fitting for a nun to move as silently as the Holy Spirit, Brother Garcilaso."

"It pleases you to be glib, I see. Is this too a virtue taught you by Mother Catalina?"

"That you must ask of her."

"Do not be insolent! Your confession will never be acceptable to God if you come before Him in arrogance of heart."

"I come to make no confession."

"Indeed? You should. You have gone unshriven too long, and are of such undeservedly haughty temperament that the tally of your sins must be overlong by this."

"I have found a new confessor, Brother Garcilaso."

"Ha! Where, in this godforsaken land? Who sets you your penances now? A satyr in minor orders? A merman turned Jesuit? A crested fireworm of Saint Dominic's Rule?"

"Saint Francis', rather."

"What? Speak up! You stand there, so demurely, your hands tucked away in the sleeves of your habit as if you were the most delicate of Mary's flowers. You forget, Sister Ana, that we know you for what you are: A familiar of demons, a consort of infidels!"

"You forget to add: a bastard."

"Would I could also forget you from existence. You disgust me. Go."

"I will not, Brother Garcilaso."

"You *will* not?"

"You will be the one to leave these rooms, not I. Why do you seek her out? You have no business here; no healthy business. Do you expect to do it so easily? She is too well guarded for that now, and when the hour of the birth comes, she shall be like a lily set about with a forest of iron thorns. So you see, it does you little good to lurk in the Jewess' apartments, awaiting the opportunity to work mischief. You shall have none. They will never permit you the solitude a murder requires."

"It would be no murder."

"What, then?"

"A cleansing. A healing."

"By fire, I suppose. You are fond of such cures."

"Laugh, then. I see where my duty lies, despite you. Praise God, a man is not so easily distracted by the gaudy trappings of this accursed palace as a woman."

"Of course not. You joy in the pale, small cell they have assigned you, sleep peacefully on only two mattresses. And that small brass-bound casket which reposes beneath your bed contains only the most austere diamonds."

"What! How did you—? If you have stolen any of—"

"Peace. It remains where you disposed it. Although if you wish to leave these rooms and make certain of it, I will never prevent you."

"Hrrmh. Your word on it will do, Sister Ana. The jewels I reserve for the benefit of your convent, after all. You measure me by your own petty heart."

"To my shame, then, holy Brother. You do so much for us. I am chastened. And for yourself? For your brethren, nothing?"

"For what I do here, Their Most Catholic Majesties and Holy Mother Church will requite me."

"Yes; I had forgotten. What is the royal fee for sanctified assassins?"

"Serpent."

"Servant."

"Of the devil."

"Of an unborn child. Of one you would sooner not see born, is that not so? . . . You are silent, Brother. Why? Do you fear the truth, or only me? You may speak. See, we are alone here."

"In God's name, I do not fear anything so low as you. This is no murder I shall do, no blood shall be upon my hands, yet I vow by the heads of all the saints, this blasphemy shall not be born!"

"You do mean to kill the baby, then."

"I do not mean to let fresh heresy see the light."

"Words. Only you could twist them so. If I listened to you long enough, you might convince me that a child's death would rejoice the heart of God. I will not listen. You have said enough. Now go, before I summon some who will make you go."

"I will go when I like; not before."

"Do you see this, Brother Garcilaso?"

"A box. Why have you been holding it inside your sleeve? What is in it?"

"Your ruin. Your words. Hear:"

. . .

"Brother Garcilaso, you do not look like a well man. I assure you, everyone reacts so the first time they hear their voices thrown back at them from this contrivance. I, myself, was horrified to learn I sounded so shrill as—"

"Witchcraft! Infamous sorcery!"

"Testimony. Or call it confession. Evidence that I may use if you so much as enter the same room as the little Jewess and her son, once he is born. I do not want your death, Brother Garcilaso, but there are creatures here as hungry for your blood as for their own promise of salvation. Steal from them the one and I will see to it that they hear this, and come to take the other."

"For this you will burn, Sister Ana."

"Not in your God's hell, Brother Garcilaso, nor in that of your many masters. I, too, do what I must. The Savior I serve will never condemn me for daring the wolf to save the lamb."

Sixteen

But I am condemned. I toy with Prester John's mysterious *contrivance* by the hour, hearing and hearing again the harsh and bitter sound of Brother Garcilaso's words, the cool self-possession of my own, and curse the arrogance that set me to confront him—when? Was it only yesterday? More than a sun has set since then. More than a night has perished.

The bubbles of worlds float and dance around me. The captive faces, bronze and copper and brown, all gape at me for release. Here at my right hand a temple glitters with a skin of gold, there a jade mask gleams. The curving skin of a magician's spell wears thinner by the minute as the pent reality of each dancing sphere burgeons, ripens, threatens to burst forth and engulf us all.

And there is no remedy. I sit upon the jeweled throne of Prester John, his body at my feet, and watch his myriad bubble-worlds drift ever farther and higher from their fallen maker's ambit. Some are still dappled with his blood.

There is much blood, so much. Outside this room,

there will be more. I cannot differentiate between the pathetic cries of the pursued, the enraged shrieks of the pursuers, the keening of those too abruptly baffled by one man's sheer heartless cruelty to do more than mourn.

I cannot watch the blood as it seeps from beneath the Nubian's huge body, a somnolent snake, a dully crimson trail like a raindrop's slow passage down a cold stone wall. I cannot watch the worlds of his making either. Each is a hovering reproach, an admonishing eye that floats and bobbles before me, bright exemplum of what it means to truly *make*. Ever and always my eyes return to take sanctuary in the sight of the pen that writes, the hand that holds it. That guides it, too? Oh, no. That would make of me more than I am, and I am no maker. This world now pays the price of my last sally into a creator's pride.

All this comes, as Mother Catalina would say, of my forgetting my place, who I am, what little I must ever be: a scribe, no more.

This I forget to my peril, and to a world's losing. I am but the vessel of testimony. I am nothing save the conduit through which the happening moments chill into the rigid fixity of words upon a page. Like the good sculptor, I make the cuts, but it is the stone's own heart that draws the chisel only so deep and no deeper. The statue dreams within the rock, waiting for the kindred force, the *other*, that with its very soul knows the dreaming statue's waking form. It is this *other* who, at the proper time, calls upon the mortal sculptor who shall be its tool and sets his hand to the task.

The pen is my tool as tool I am to that unnamed *other*.

Ah, the elusive *other*, whose very anonymity plays the Grand Inquisitor, the master whose hand holds me twisting slowly above the flames. Being human, I ache to tame it with a name. An angel, might it be? The heathen peoples who did not know God, called on beings very like to angels. I have read of she-gods, nine in all, who bring the words and the music and the dance and all the arts to birth, giving shape and sense to what before was only pure idea. Whatever the entity that chooses to work its will through me—angel or spirit less authoritatively blessed—they are still as much tools of a greater being as I am tool of theirs, as this ragged pen is tool of mine.

I suppose I must name it God. That, or burn for it. I do not wish to burn.

So I, poor instrument—poor *contrivance* of whatever being's making—I shall write. It is what I do. It is what I am. It is all to which I ought aspire. It is my poor shadow of the true creation. And perhaps it is a shadow forged of steel, in the end. If I do not fill this sheet with what I have witnessed, it must be as if it never had been. Others cause; I seal their causes with an inky immortality.

If it were only so! If I could but—*unhappen* is no honest Castillian word, yet it is the sorry best I can do to name my desire. Yes, if I could but *unhappen* what has passed here within less than a day's time—if I might deny past events their actuality by refusing to chronicle them here—O Lord, for that boon I would give more than my soul's service! I would write it all away, and then forever lay aside my pen.

But I am the scribe. A demon named me so, but the naming is not the making. Demons are in the habit of recognizing the raw truth that lurks behind each human face, but they do not put it there. My honor as scribe will not allow me to do more than offer up what is and what has been. And what might someday be? Pride again. The veil between this hour and the next is not to be raised by anything so fragile as a penpoint, though whittled from a gryphon's wing with a knife of gold.

I still prefer seagull quills, myself.

Besides, I have lifted too many curtains. Always I find a grinning skull behind each one.

So it was, and so I must preserve it as it was: I was sleeping when the alarm came. My dreams were full of Brother Garcilaso, beaten and bested by my ready words at every turn. Phrase by phrase, I pared him down, my words lifting away first skin, then flesh, then sinew, then scraping through bloody bone into the marrow before he screamed.

The scream went on, too long, too loud. It roused me from slumber before I realized it was nothing I had dreamed. Then *la Zagala* burst in upon me before I could do more than sit up in bed.

"Come at once!" she cried. I never saw her so pale.

I followed. The palace halls were a clatter of hooves and talons over sleek marble and iridescent mosaic. All of the torches licked away the night with fragrant tongues of fire. Exquisite monsters swarmed chittering through the air. One snagged itself by pearly blue claws in my hair. The gypsy wench's summons did not leave me time enough to throw any manner of covering over my head, for shame's sake. The creature bit me with a toothless, rubbery beak when I set it free.

We ran until we reached the little Jewess' apartments. The very rooms seemed distended with the sound of mourning within, a keening wail that swelled the monumental doors containing it. Twin goat-footed men crouched crumpled beside the doorposts, weeping over broken silver spears. They did not even challenge us as *la Zagala* threw open the portal they were supposed to guard.

What use to guard? It was over.

The rope was silk. I know, because I ran the braided length of it through my fingers after they cut her down. It was pale yellow, the color of a parched winter sun, or a noblewoman's plaited hair. There being no exposed beams, she had cast the anchoring loop over the projecting branch of a jeweled pear tree.

The babe was dead within her. The lady Rasha said so, but her lord Zamiz the Unaccountably Repulsive would not believe her. I wish he might have had the kindness to announce his plans. Given the choice, I would have hurried from the chamber before his fingernails sliced through robe and skin and flesh, opening the silent womb.

There was no blame. She had been alone when she did it. She had just returned from a slow, wordless progress down the great hall whose unglazed windows overlook the gardens. The sweet air of dusk seemed to have an enlivening influence on her, or so her weeping handmaidens averred as they gasped out this testimony. She had even drawn away from their steadying hands and gone of her own will to stand beneath a window's pointed arch, seeming to hearken to the sounds of late birdsong from the greenery below.

The winged women swore that it was most wonderful, the effect of that brief stroll. As she stood by the window, her eyes had gone bright, her chin jerked up, her sealed lips parted like one who suddenly wakes. She turned to them transformed, and demanded to be taken back to her suite. Once there, she had dismissed them all from the room, most firmly. They saw no harm in it. Their hearts were too joyed by the fact that she had chosen to find her voice once more.

Although they left her alone, at her command, that did not mean they left her unprotected. Her attendants were but a door's thickness away, and they were scrupulous to see that no one entered to disturb their lady. Prester John's express commands were quite specific as to who was least welcome in those rooms. One of the little Jewess' distraught maidservants swore by the soul she had lost that Brother Garcilaso, Mother Catalina, and the rest were all in the tamarind garden; had been there, in fact, since well before the last time anyone saw the little Jewess alive.

"In the tamarind garden," Zamiz repeated. His ponderous head moved slowly from side to side, contemplating the marvel of these beings' innocence. Although I do not claim to know the entire plan of Prester John's palace, nor do I presume knowledge of the location of every garden its magnificence contains, one look at the face of Zamiz the Unaccountably Repulsive told me precisely which bowery precinct may be viewed from the unglazed windows of the great hall.

The testimony of the little Jewess' milk-skinned maids was truth itself, and just as palatable. Zamiz clenched his fists so that the nails poked through the palms and sprouted like horns at the base of his wrists. Then he spread his bleeding hands wide enough to sweep the trembling creatures up and crush them like a handful of dead leaves. Their blood had the delicate smell of almonds. In innocence, in ignorance, there is no saving grace.

The lady Rasha did not try to stop her lord, being wise. Instead, she called for a basin of water. She washed the dead child and wrapped it in a length of gold-shot gossamer before laying it in its mother's arms. Male or female? I had no stomach to pry. Death makes no such distinctions, and Death rules more than a pot of ink and a pen. I will not rise above my betters.

Prester John arrived just as a troop of clawed and tusked wildmen dragged in Brother Garcilaso and the others. The priest-king's face was dry, smooth as a river-bed stone. My sisters sobbed without tears and moaned as if the little Jewess' forfeit labor had devolved upon them. Our confessor shuddered in his captors' grasp, but I saw a fearsome look of triumph on his pinched and whitened lips.

Seventeen

At Prester John's direction, we were all conducted to this room, where the throne stands, where I now sit. A multitude of his subjects crammed the chamber, that now echoes so eerily. Zamiz himself, heeding his lord's behest, kept the mob from surging forward to crush the accused.

I cowered behind the throne, fearing all, seeing all, no less a captive than my sisters in Christ and my confessor. Prester John placed me there, ever the scribe, to record faithfully what came to pass. In the shadows, my presence went unnoted, while I noted all. My nostrils filled with the bitter stench of galbanum, the heady seduction of myrrh, the homely smell of heavily besweated wool. Peeping around the right side of the throne, I fixed my gaze on the enormous blue carbuncle gemming Prester John's forefinger. He wore no other ornament that night, and the light streaming from the jewel's perfect facets seemed to be the only thing left pure in all the world. I clung to the light as to hope.

"Come forward, Brother Garcilaso," said Prester

John. The Franciscan's captors gave him a shove that sent him to his knees. I heard him cry out in pain as his hands struck the sharp edge of the dais steps. Zamiz the Unaccountably Repulsive was pleased to laugh, a sound bereft of any joy.

Prester John raised his jeweled hand. "Silence," he said. "This is no time for laughter." I could count the folds of fat at the back of his neck as he lowered his gaze to where Brother Garcilaso huddled. "Well?" he asked. "Will you tell us?"

"I have nothing to tell," Brother Garcilaso returned, so that the most addle-brained fool would know it was a lie.

"I will sound him." Zamiz the Unaccountably Repulsive loomed over my confessor like a black, storm-conjured wave. Having seen what he could do, I came near to wishing Brother Garcilaso the mercy of a swift death.

But Prester John would have matters otherwise. He called off the demon in a few terse words. Zamiz subsided, muttering. He reached inside the shadows of his sleeves and brought out a single shining sphere. Oily golden swirls swam across its surface as he let it roll from hand to hand.

"You shall be safe, Brother." Prester John's voice sounded distant as the dragon-haunted peaks through which our caravan had climbed. "Safe haven, rich haven, a golden world delivered up into your care. Souls also. Many souls, for you to be their agent of salvation. Their gratitude will be as honey poured from the heart of the rock, lapping you in sweetness." He set the ball to twirling on his fingertip. The blue carbuncle winked beneath it. "All this you shall have, Brother Garcilaso, as payment simple for the truth you know."

Brother Garcilaso straightened his shoulders. The courage of a man with nothing left to lose stiffened his spine and taught his tongue insolence. "Is that what you offer me?" He did not use even the most modest of Prester John's honorifics, to give his reply the mask of courtesy, but addressed him baldly. "Captivity in one of your pet worlds? I should like that, indeed! Trade the truth I know for the illusion of a safe, rich life, the tending of so many souls?" His laugh was brittle as an insect's shell. "Illusions all, soul and substance! You will not beguile me with such bait."

I saw Prester John's huge body sag between the armrests of his throne. "I shall not. And yet there are many men willing to trade what they imagine is truth for what they know is illusion." The golden ball bobbed lightly on his fingertip, then took gentle flight, hovering on its master's breath. "I do not make empty offers, Brother," said Prester John. "No more do I lay claim to powers which I do not possess. These worlds I show you, they were never mine in the making."

From my place behind the throne, Brother Garcilaso's skeptical expression was plain to see. "I thought—" he began.

Prester John forestalled him. "You thought what many thought, my most faithful subjects among them. I will give you the truth of it, in good faith, in hopes of your repaying me in kind." Here he took breath, and the golden sphere spun on.

"When the older world shook off its magic, herded the

creatures of shadow from its shores, I journeyed in the van, seeking the land where they might dwell in peace, awaiting salvation. We came to these lands, but we were not the first. Others were in possession. I could not read the souls of the men who had prime claim to the realm I desired. I could not see whether their hearts were warm and wide enough to share their lands with my poor persecuted flock."

He drew forth a second sphere to float beside the first. "I was pressed; so many were coming after me, desperate for a place of refuge! I thought it best to ask nothing, for fear of hearing the wrong answer. I did not wish to chance it. And so I set my spells around those firstdwellers here, sealing each people safe within a world sacrosanct to their own ways. A world shut off from all differences, all other modes of thought, all disparate paths to the throne of God!" His voice climbed the heights, then fell like a bird surprised by the crossbow bolt beneath its breast. "A garden enclosed, a mind well sealed, content."

Brother Garcilaso hearkened, and gazed hungrily now at the airborne globe. His tongue moistened his lips, tasting a promised Paradise, a land where there would be no way to reach Our Lord's ear but through His servant, Brother—no, Prester Garcilaso! Still, he hesitated, asking, "But are the souls within—the souls you promise me—are they never aware of being so contained?"

Prester John shook his head. "They have never noticed their isolation."

Other bubbles of light drifted from Prester John's sleeves, climbing invisible spiral stairs before him.

"Sometimes they touch, the worlds that I have saved and set aside. Sometimes I think I see phantoms pass from one into the next, as a silk thread pierces its way through a strand of pearls. It was always my intent to free them all, some day; the day of our salvation. I would tap each sphere like an egg and hatch a captive people back into the light."

Prester John's sigh spun the floating worlds like dead leaves in a millpond eddy. "So you see, Brother Garcilaso, I make no false offer here. The souls within these spheres are as real, as human as yours or mine. You shall enter the world of your choice by my will—the Sisters too, should they desire as much—and remain there quite safe from any action of myself or my subjects."

All this while, Sister Angustias was staring at the spinning sphere nearest her. I saw steep-sided buildings sloping up to gold-decked temples at their summits. Brilliant hues of gems and feathers and fine clothes were everywhere. Sister Angustias' lips hung open like a hake's mouth. "Anywhere?" she asked. "Into any of these worlds, and for no more than the truth? We shall be safe?"

"You have my word," Prester John replied. He lifted his head and surveyed the faces of his subjects, massed before him. I saw what he saw, though I doubt the sight turned his blood a tithe so cold.

Sister Angustias opened and closed her mouth repeatedly, though no sensible sound escaped. Her long white fingers knotted themselves into a tangle of frantic thought, intertwined with her precious rosary. "And if—and if we do not speak?" she asked.

"Then your safety remains your own concern," said Prester John. "May you guard it as well as you hoard the truth."

"*He* told her!" Angustias' shriek raked my ears quite raw. The pearl rosary swung back and forth at the end of the finger she pointed at Brother Garcilaso, a hangman's noose fit for a priest-king. "We were in the garden, walking the paths, saying our devotions at compline. Suddenly Brother Garcilaso stopped, looked up! He saw her standing under the pointed arch of an open window."

"And spoke to her." Prester John's words held the weariness of one who knew the worst.

"One word—only one! I overheard. It was not more than a whisper. He said—"

"*Enough!*" Mother Catalina roared with all an ancient lion's rage when the cubs grow too fractious and forget their master. Her crabbed claw struck down Angustias' elegant hand, knocked the rosary from it. The silk broke, the pearls clattered away. "Treacherous child, will you see us all die? He will take your truth and use it to destroy this holy man, who is our only hope!" She dealt Angustias a pair of cheek-brightening slaps and rushed to fling her meager body over Brother Garcilaso's shoulders, a skeleton cloak. "Spare him, my lord! One word alone, that was all he uttered. Can you destroy a man for so little? Can you prove it was a word intended for that cursed, mad girl's ears and not merely a thing she happened to overhear? Can you hold this saintly man responsible for so much, on so little basis?"

Prester John stroked his chin. "That," he said slowly, "would depend upon the word."

"Let the word be death!" *la Zagala* shouted from the mob of monsters. Many took up her cry.

Prester John was hard pressed to silence them. A gesture proved insufficient. The bobbing globes shook within their several orbits as he called upon greater spells, jelling the air around those creatures too willing to follow the gypsy wench's call for blood. It was a thing of wonder, to see beasts scaled and semi-human moving sluggishly, as if the clear atmosphere embracing them had turned to bog.

This accomplished, he turned again to Brother Garcilaso. "I tire," he said. "I cannot tell you honestly whether I shall lift the spell now holding your enemies because I must or because I feel like it. Speak the word, Brother. Speak it just as it was spoken within *her* hearing. Add nothing, explain nothing. And do it now."

Brother Garcilaso tightened his mouth stubbornly for a moment, then appeared to reconsider. He put aside Mother Catalina's bony clasp and raised himself from his knees.

"*Remember.*"

Eighteen

"Remember."

There it lies, trickled from my pen, a word; no more, no less, just as Prester John had bidden him speak it. It sounded no more impressive coming from Brother Garcilaso's mouth than it now looks, inscribed upon this page.

But then: *"Remember,"* echoed Prester John, and the sound of it was foul smoke pouring from his lips, a sooty scroll of linked letters like those which stream from the mouths of woodcut devils. The word sucked substance from the air, resolved itself into a crystal sphere like all the rest presently hovering at Prester John's beck. Where those were worlds of light, this was a world of darkness. Alas, not so dark that all present might not see what it contained.

Remember. A dungeon cell, and a girl scarce out of childhood. She knows that they mean to kill her, but first they will hurt her. Why? What has she done? The others counsel her to be brave, to be true, to be righteous for the sanctification of the Name. What does she know of truth or righteousness? God, who is the source of all, has abandoned her. All she knows is the terror, the naked fear.

Remember. Her companions are taken from the cell, one by one. They return broken, but silent. Why? She knows that when her turn comes she will shriek, she will cry, she will not be able to stop crying. And is that a smile she sees? Impossible. Knowing what she knows, fearing what she fears, she will never smile again.

Remember. Because she must remember a bargain badly made, a cowardly pact undertaken to save herself from what her comrades suffer now so willingly, so proudly. She has no pride. She has only the desire to survive unhurt. That was why the bargain. That was why, when she was first made prisoner of the Holy Office, she gave herself like any common whore to the jailor who swore he would let her go. He did not. Instead he passed her along to the men who later would break the bones of her fellow prisoners, the men who would build the scaffold and pile up the wood beneath, the men who would thrust their torches deep into the kindling and laugh while the flames ran with melting flesh.

Remember. Remember the long months of waiting, the months when her companions are taken from the cell again and again for questioning, while she is taken from it for another purpose.

Remember. Remember the moment when she first discovers that her womb carries a child.

Remember. Remember how the men all laugh when she tells them, and none claims fatherhood of a little bastard Jew. Even while her belly swells beneath the loose drape of the yellow *sanbenito*, they use her as before. Will it harm the babe? They tell her not to mind that. All of them reassure her that her troubled thoughts for the child will be laid to rest soon enough. Fire is a fine, final counselor.

Remember. Remember the miracle, the rescue, the others left behind to die bravely for the sanctification of the Name while she—the unworthy, the jailors' cowardly whore—is saved.

Remember. Remember how they hail her in this alien land as a vessel of salvation, blessed the fruit of her womb. But what savior can be born wrapped in the flesh of her imperfect flesh? She will mother forth sin, not salvation; so she believes with all the passion that the world has left her. She knows the beliefs of her former jailors well, and knows she will be no virgin mother. These otherworldly beings who laud her for bringing them the gift of souls redeemed, how will they suffer on account of her and her past failings? She will betray them as she has betrayed her own people, out of cowardly self-love. They do not know the truth. They cannot know. She forces it from her with all her might, and for a time the mute kindness of oblivion shields her.

Until a voice pierces through and bids: *Remember.*

Until, remembering, she realizes that there is only one sure way to truly forget.

My heart felt harder, blacker than the sphere that thrust a dead girl's memories into our minds. Heavier than the weight of sin is that of culpability. Remember? I remember all too well. And if my human memory fails, I have the evidence of Prester John's *contrivance* to accuse me. Who can say but that my taunts were what turned Brother Garcilaso's brain from outright murder to the subtler path whose fruit so lately swung, ripe-ready, by a golden cord from a jeweled pear tree's branch?

Had I cultivated wisdom where pride took root, I might have let him try his worst. Brute force against the little Jewess would have been his death, not hers. Instead, I stepped into the skin of his *other:* His the deed, but mine the inspiration. I turned him to the path of words, and like all good churchmen, he was their master.

I caught Brother Garcilaso's eye. Clear triumph shone beneath the pouchy lid. The wolf had won; the lamb was dead, and I the one who led it to the slaughter.

Whatever Prester John's folk did to my most saintly confessor, he would die with the sweet knowledge that worse must come to me.

Prester John rose from his throne and caught the dark sphere in both hands. He twisted his fingers tightly around it, and wrung out tears enough to rival the ocean sea's eternal grief. Streams of salt water flowed down his massive arms. When he parted his hands, the globe was gone.

"You have given me all I asked," he said to Brother Garcilaso. "For this, I thank you." He covered his face with hands still running salt with brine and, for the first time since the death of babe and mother, wept.

Brother Garcilaso yelped for attention. "Wait! I have given you your truth. Make good your bargain."

Even from behind the throne I could see how Prester John's fat cheeks were a solid wash of tears. "So it shall be," he said, to the strident protests of every being—beast or human or both—in the throne room. "I have given you my word."

He swept the air with his hands and the twirling globes fell into procession. "Choose," he said. "Choose well."

I saw my confessor and my sisters move towards them, eyes aglitter, fingers outstretched to grasp the brightest world. Mother Catalina and Sister Angustias crowded after Brother Garcilaso, who yearned towards that world of glittering temples, jade-masked priests, and swaying rainbow plumes. A touch of greed-trembling fingers to the bubble's straining skin, and they vanished, sucked through the fragile membrane of whorled gold.

A hellish roar of protest issued from the throats of all of Prester John's subjects who witnessed their escape. The sheer volume of sound was a tempest that beat back my remaining sisters from the globes they would have grasped. Their robes whipped out in the storm of outrage like belling sails to drag them over the world's edge. Rage burned high, searing away the tenuous hold of the priest-king's magic. The jellied air liquefied in the momentary flash of cleansing flame, and when the lightning died, the creatures felt their freedom. They surged forward, making straight for Sister Elena, Sister Incarnación, and old Sister Magdalena.

This pen is unequal to describe a wave compounded of every nightmare vision ever dreamed—scaled, furred, taloned, fanged, belching flame, stink, venom. Let my shame record that I gave a small cry of abject fear and curled myself into the tightest of balls, willing myself invisible if I could not will myself away. I heard the rumble and clatter and pounding of their paws and hooves and feet over the throne room floor. I heard the screams of my Sisters in Christ, and the shout of Prester John: "Stop, my children, my own! I tell you you *are* saved, all!" There was more, but the thunder of their onslaught struck the steps of the throne and gushed upwards until the mad cacophony swirled everywhere around me and Prester John's voice was swallowed whole.

And through all the mad uproar, came a young voice— no one's, someone's—and a high, excited call heard against the mewling of gulls, the creaking of spars, and the freshening wind that blows through a ship's topmost rigging:

"*Land! Land!*"

Nineteen

Land?

I almost lifted my head then, to seek the demon who had pierced the mob's roar with this, the most incongruous of sounds, a sailor's gladdest hail. Against the crimson starred dark of my eyelids I saw three ships, and heard again the happy cry of *Land!* before the angry din rushed back to smother every sound but its own blood-cry.

Then, by small degrees, it ebbed. The fury passed, the white rage of sound around me grew gradually softer, pulling away. I felt it go, as one who lies buried deep beneath a fall of rock senses her rescuers begin to roll aside the first stones, far above. In time, I gained the heart to uncurl my body and lift up my eyes.

The throne was empty; the throne room was not. At the foot of the steps *la Zagala* knelt, the point of a dagger glimmering between her breasts. She said, "If you take another step nearer, I will end this."

She did not speak to me. I do not believe she knew I was there. It was at Prester John she leveled her threats.

The Nubian king stood poised with one foot upon a marble tread, the other hovering above the next step down from the throne. He balanced there, between breath and breath, as delicately as any butterfly. The spheres of his summoning clouded around him, and in his voice came the tremulous flutter of wings.

"You will not do this, my child," he said. Lovers could not implore a favor more tenderly, more fearful of refusal. "Lay aside the blade."

"Why?" The gypsy girl's harsh challenge crackled like a flint-struck spark. "Because you'll promise me some grand reward if I do? I've taken your word too often!"

"Will none of you listen?" I saw the blue carbuncle twinkle in and out of sight as Prester John wrung his hands. "Will you desert me, like the rest, unheard, unhearing?"

"What is there to hear?" *la Zagala* demanded. "She is dead! *Dead*, and the baby with her, and all of our salvation with them!" Her anger chilled to bitterness. "If we were ever to have salvation from such a source." I had to lean against the back of the throne to hear her mutter, "—no virgin. Tell me that you didn't know."

Prester John collapsed heavily on the steps of the throne in an outrush of air and a rustle of draperies. "I will not lie to you," he said.

"You won't lie to me any further, you mean," the gypsy sneered. "Your word was all I had to name her virgin. I trusted it so well that I never thought to prove or disprove it for myself. And I had the opportunity!" Her hands shifted slightly on the dagger's hilt. Her dark hair fell forward in trailing fringes as she bowed her head over the blade, intent on finishing what she had begun.

"Child, child, punish me some other way for my deceit." Prester John's entreaty did not move the blade a hairbreadth from the gypsy's breast. Still he persisted: "To take the life that is God's gift—to take it by violence even from your own bosom—that will lose you more than life."

"What more?" *La Zagala* tossed her head and spat as near the priest-king's feet as she might. "My soul? But I forfeited that long ago, if I ever had it to begin with. Has a slave a soul, or is it her master's? What about a whore? One who hasn't even got the right to say yes or no? One who has pacted with your own pet demons, my lord?" These last words she uttered with all the scorn her heart could hold.

Prester John would have replied, but she did not give him the chance. "I'm a worse gull than all your miserable, empty-headed monsters. Poor brutes, so innocent! Blank walls, where you could write any spew and have those creatures believe it! But I knew the world's way. I knew, and in spite of that, I believed you when you promised me redemption."

Now she was crying without tears. Hard sobs racked her body. Words tore their way from her throat as if each would bring up blood in its wake. "Where is the new world you promised us, Prester John? Where's the saving grace that was supposed to wipe away all differences between slave and master, low and high, woman and man? The ships will be here soon, and all their brave crew. What are we to do? Greet them with open arms, or just fling ourselves in the dust at their feet? They'll bring us to that sooner or later, you know. They'll have no qualms about it. To them, I'll be about as human as a goat-horned man, or an eagle-headed lion, or one of those webfooted merfolk. Not a soul in the lot! Not human at all! And for that reason alone, fair game." She looked at the knife again. "No, thank you. I know that tune too well to dance to it again."

She cocked back the blade, the better to bury it in her chest. The carbuncle flashed, and blue fire froze hand and blade immobile. *La Zagala* bared her teeth like a cornered wolf. "Let me go."

Prester John shook his head, refusing. "I will not have another death to my account. First you will listen."

La Zagala was not disposed to do so. "Your powers won't survive the moment when those ships beach. I can wait. For once, I'll have a choice."

"You can have more than that." Prester John no longer addressed her gently. There was a measure of my father's steel in his voice. "You will have truth." This promise sounded like foretold punishment.

"Know, then, what I know for fact, what I learned from the mouths of those winged messengers who first gave me my mission," he told her. "You and the others, you are as human as any work of His hands, formed with as much love. Because you are so human, you would never accept your souls on my word alone. I know; I have tried to teach you this many times before. None would believe; not without proof. Why do you never require such stringent proof of your own perdition? *That* you swallow whole! Does damnation reassure you that you matter in the world? Are you so eager to measure the significance of your small lives by God's wrath rather than His love? A sign! A sign that was no more truly necessary for your salvation than that dead girl's supposed virginity, yet still you would insist upon it. Well, I tried to give you your *sign!*"

"A sign," the gypsy wench repeated. "A fine sign, to swing back and forth at a rope's end, like a tavern board." Her knuckles whitened as she strained to break the magic bonds keeping the dagger from her heart. "You'll pardon me if I still try to prove things my own way."

I heard strange words murmured from the priest-king's lips. The dagger rippled in and out of reality. *La Zagala* hissed a protest. "Damn you, you won't take this from me. Would it be easier to let me die if I were an infant? Would one more death added to that old score matter much to you?"

It was then I heard a voice—shrill, like a piglet's squeal; piping as a bat's squeak—a voice I knew and hated for my own, crying out, "Throw that in his face again, and I swear by all holy, I'll separate skin from soul for you!"

The gypsy snickered. "Leave it to the Church to take the practical way. I should've let you examine that poor girl for the virgin's mark on shipboard that night. We'd all have been spared more than a measure of grief. She and her baby, they were just part of that old mountebank's show, a streetcorner juggler's dazzle to distract the crowd while his partner picks their pockets. A *sign* to make us accept what he claims has always been so. Of course we believe him. He never lies."

I nearly slipped and tumbled down the steps in my hurry to reach her, but the same spell that kept the dagger frozen in her hand prevented me from seizing her by the shoulders and shaking her like a rag. "You are a fine one to speak of believing! If you and the rest would have believed him to begin—believed him on faith, demanding no proof—none of this would have proved needful! The deaths of mother and child are on your account, not his!"

She laughed at me.

"Go to the window, Sister Ana," she said. "There you will see a sign to remember always."

I must have frowned in puzzlement, but I went. *La Zagala* did not understate her case. I will indeed remember what I then saw for as long as God gives me breath. No, I will carry the memory even to the gates of heaven.

The sky was dark with dragons. Anything with wings was taking to the air, soaring as far from those shores as it could go. In the distance I saw the spell-built cliffs rumbling down into violet dust, the enchanted woodlands parching until leaf and branch were insubstantial as a breath of sand. The land reverberated with the thunder of countless feet, and I saw the herds of wondrous beings stampeding away.

I turned from the window and told of what I had seen. My expression must have matched Prester John's for shock. *La Zagala* found it all most entertaining. "The ocean's a froth of panicked sea-beasts, too," she said, glorying in our distress. "Whatever has wings or fins or feet is using them to get safely far from here. All of them are running away."

"But why?" Prester John's voice crumpled to a pathetic whisper. "Why do they flee? Where do they think they can go?"

"Where?" *la Zagala* echoed. "Anywhere, so long as it's hidden from the sight of men. Back to the hell that birthed them. Back to whatever pit vomited up so many soulless shells. Why? Because this little life is all they have, with only emptiness to come after. They won't risk losing it. Should they? If men who've got some hope of heaven can be cowardly, then terror's the very birthright of the soulless. For them, death ends all. If even one of us owned the soul you claim, why hasn't the God who gave it seen fit to speak from it Himself and tell us not to fear?"

Prester John pushed himself up clumsily from the steps. "Is that what you require, child? A miracle? Still?"

La Zagala grinned. "Miracles are for saints and charlatans. Gypsies make bargains."

"Very well. So be it." Prester John beckoned to me. "Go back to your place, Sister Ana. Take up your pen and paper. Write as I dictate." I obeyed, a good daughter of the Rule, clambering back up the steps while he called out behind me, "You shall be the witness to the terms of this—*bargain.*" I could tell he found the word to be a foul taste in his mouth.

He descended the last of the throne steps and stood beside the kneeling woman, hands folded over his bulging belly. "A bargain needs two sides, and we make two bargains here: One between me and this lady, one with God."

I laid down my pen. It is Satan who traffics in the marketplace. One does not call upon the Lord to haggle; this much I know, though Brother Garcilaso did his best to sermonize God into nothing more than a universal This-for-That, and my confessor His favored agent.

Prester John heard the click of the quill set aside. He waved for me to take it up again. "Sister Ana, yours is to record, not to question." He spoke a truth I recognized. I retrieved my pen. He nodded approval, then spoke to *la Zagala*. "For our bargain, lady, if I give you proof of what you seek, what will you give to me?"

The gypsy's bright eyes sparkled with cunning. "You can name that price."

"So I shall," he answered. He drew the blue carbuncle from his hand and set it on the floor before her. "My price is high: The assumption of my mantle. My children shall be yours—to seek out, to comfort, to banish their fears, to gather home—" His head tilted back, his eyes closed. "—to teach where I have failed, that their souls' existence and saving rests in no hands but their own. Agreed?"

"Agreed," said *la Zagala*. She spoke lightly, like a man who incurs a debt he knows he will never repay.

He bid me write that down, adding that the ring would be seal and sign for that portion of the pact. His lips quivered with a wistful smile when he said *sign*.

"And now for the other portion of this bargain we make here," he continued. His eyes opened to the ceiling of the throne room where painted stars shone with unnatural light.

I would not record the terms of his second bargain. Although these chronicles of mine may ultimately come to rest in the heart of a flame, I would not chance it that someone else might see the words Prester John used to deal with the Almighty. Let this suffice: That if his subjects owned nothing but the flesh, then *la Zagala*'s dagger might be free to pierce that flesh; that if an immortal soul also beat beneath the wings of a dragon and the hairy bosom of a satyr, then the gypsy's steel might only end a seeming immortality.

When he was done, he asked me, "Do you have that?" I nodded. "Good," he said. "Now record exactly what you shall see and hear."

I obeyed. What passed then was very simple. A word, and the bonds on *la Zagala* were lifted. Her eyes flashed with that realization. Then quickly, furtively, as if she were a midnight thief who must snatch away what he desires before the nightwatch can blink, she thrust the dagger into her heart—

—and stared at the hilt that bruised her breasts but pulled away and left her whole, alive.

But a scarlet fountain bubbled up into the hands Prester John cupped against his chest, and he measured his own length at *la Zagala*'s feet.

Twenty

The gypsy screamed and bolted from the room. I remained. I had much to record. I do not know how much of it I had accomplished when I became aware of the presence of another. It was the lady Rasha's lord, Zamiz the Unaccountably Repulsive. He was a gust of desert wind at my back, a smell of brimstone, commingled with the uncanny scent of cinnamon and orange flowers.

I thought I was to die, yet all I feared was that my writing should go unfinished. Then he spoke, and it was not to bid me make one last prayer.

He said: "I was the first she found. I have heard." He looked to where Prester John's body lay and added, "He always said that truth was not cheaply purchased." The demon lowered his eyes and touched his forehead in a gesture of respect for the fallen king. To me he said, "For my late-come soul's sake, Sister Ana, I will take you home."

So now I wait while Zamiz the Unaccountably Repulsive flies through the palace seeking certain knowledge of my remaining (if they do remain) sisters. While I wait, I find it easier to glance at the floating worlds of Prester John's last summoning. Zamiz has told me to gaze while I can. The cry of land precedes the Genoese's landfall by relatively little. Once the first keel grates over the sand, that sound will tear open as many of these globes as it takes to fill a new world.

Therefore I observe while I may. I find the one into which Brother Garcilaso, Mother Catalina, and Sister Angustias passed most fascinating. You can see everything within the sphere, whose small size nonetheless refuses to require all the scurrying forms within to accept a uniform miniaturization. Some things defy natural law, in a passion to be witnessed.

They stand in the midst of a marketplace greater than any I have ever seen. The natives are aghast, stricken open-mouthed with astonishment by their sudden presence. Some kneel. Brother Garcilaso's smile is as wide as Sister Angustias' as her eyes sweep the compass of this vast and opulent land which I now cup in the palm of my hand. Mother Catalina too is happy. She clings to Brother Garcilaso, her sere lips moving rapidly. I cannot hear what sounds pass within the sphere I hold, but I imagine she is chirruping on like some demented cricket (in purest Castilian, no less), telling all who will listen that she is a godsend. The natives turn blank faces to her, uncomprehending, yet she nitters on.

Obviously it has never crossed her mind that some folk speak only French.

The other globes are drifting away, borne on a breeze that steals into the throne room as the light of day steals across the tiled and marbled floors. The torches have all burnt out to stubs of fragrant smoke. Somewhere a caravel is coming to rest at anchor. A boat is being lowered. Before that boat comes in to shore, these captive worlds will crack and spill out their long-guarded treasures. Where shall each alight? I do not know these western lands well enough to say. Will the Admiral of the Ocean-Sea stand astonished to be greeted by Brother Garcilaso, priest and king?

That is not a good thought. The Genoese comes in the name of my sovereigns, Their Most Catholic Majesties. It would not be an act of loyalty to allow a mere Franciscan to lay claim to what might be theirs. Why, he might even bring the Church to stand behind him and ratify his claim! Think, too, of the unholy temptation so much wealth and power bring. His very soul imperiled . . . no. I love him too dearly to let that happen, and I am also a good daughter of Castille and León.

So I shake the ball, while yet it remains in my hand. They feel it, inside. Brother Garcilaso has gone whiter than Sister Angustias' linen. Mother Catalina has tumbled into a marketplace basket that holds—can it be?—I have seen many butcher shops and know what is rumored of meat-pie sellers, but never have I seen one that vended such recognizably human wares so openly. Ah, what a world!

The natives no longer kneel. They no longer smile, nor regard my confessor with awe. They are angry. They appear to be telling him something in very definite tones. Each one of them looks like a mother who admonishes her child not to repeat an especially mischievous action.

Brother Garcilaso replies, wearing just the look such a child would assume who promises its mother that it will never do *that* again.

I give the ball another shake, the way small boys poke sticks into beehives.

I dream I hear the buzz of their voices, but that is only my fancy. They are gesturing. They demand something of Garcilaso, who makes soothing motions with his hands, his face struggling to retrieve that lost expression of bland reassurance. I recognize the gestures he now uses, static accompaniments to every sermon he ever preached whose ultimate message was *You are all doomed unless you place your trust in me.* He is a very effective speaker, especially when you do not understand a word he is saying. The twists and grimaces of his egg-smooth face are in themselves a weighty argument. So now. Some of the dark-skinned people are falling back to their knees.

This time I shake the globe until it rattles. I hope I have not broken anything I did not intend.

Once they regain their feet from this quake, no one kneels to Brother Garcilaso. A towering mask cleaves the crowd. Painted and tattooed hands seize the Franciscan's smooth cheeks. How curious. The mask seems discontented by my confessor's lack of beard. It is almost as if the stability of the ground were tied to the roots of Brother Garcilaso's nonexistent whiskers.

Are those ropes? Poor Mother Catalina! Poor Sister Angustias! They are dragged off one way, Brother Garcilaso another. He should be glad. The women are carried away to some part of the market I cannot see, tilt the globe how I will, but him they take straight to the steps of the temple.

I watch as long as I may, counting the paces of his ascent. Other masks wait at the summit, behind a stone table, gloriously carved, darkly streaked in the sun. Something black glitters high as my confessor mounts the final platform. I cannot see his lips, to tell whether he is praying. A confessor who would forget to confess his own sins? I devoutly hope he will remember.

The sphere tugs urgently from my hand, shoots across the air like a comet, sails freely out the window. I mourn to see it go.

Not for long. Here is Zamiz, and with him Sister Elena, Sister Incarnación, and Sister Magdalena too. She is the only one of them all still smiling and still sane.

Zamiz tells me that the ship awaits.

Twenty-one

Ink in a cracked cup and a quill cut from the tail of one of the convent's geese—how I have come down in the world since being named Mother Ana *de las Descalzas de la Sangre Santa!* At least I do not have to rely upon the convent stores to procure my paper. That much remains my private miracle.

I am still the scribe, albeit much risen in terms of mundane status since my return . . . how many years ago? Time's scythe has had its edge fairly blunted whenever it comes up against the walls of this holy house. Any who doubt this need only ask my dear spiritual daughters to cite the precise day on which they discovered that Mother Catalina had gone to her reward and that I had been elevated to my present office. One and all, they will refer all inquiries to the written record of our house, which in itself has become a shocking lacework of lacunae and irrelevancies unbefitting the attentive chronicler. Even I find it difficult to recall the exact date of my promotion, although we all are in agreement that it came to pass in the Year of Our Lord 1492.

This circumstance is very entertaining to those kohl-eyed phantoms who yet haunt our inner precincts, for I hear their soft, sweet laughter whispering beneath the shadowed archways. Yes, they are still here, all the ghostly Moorish ladies. No burning was sufficient to banish them, thanks be to God. I would not have them go, although I know that their continued tenancy would have driven Mother Catalina wild. Perhaps it is *because* I know this that I welcome them.

I am of course very punctilious as to the tending of my predecessor's grave, and that of Sister Angustias which lies beside it. Memory serves none but me when details of this sad double interment are called to mind. No one can recollect much of the obsequies, although every member of our house vows she was present. So they were.

And if there was but a single coffin, massive enough to contain his earthly shell, but needing two common plots of ground to encompass his eternal resting place? . . . *Ah, no!* my daughters would cry, if offered such a suggestion. *There are two markers above the graves, not one, and the names are clear to see!* (Fortunate for them that the agency which transported that kingly coffin here remained less clear to their eyes. Zamiz the Unaccountably Repulsive is not a good seeing for the unprepared.) Then, the irrefutable argument: *If it were otherwise, it would not be written so! Can you not read?*

I must confess that it was I who taught these innocents to place such blind reliance in the truth immutable of the written word. The spotty convent records notwithstanding, we have managed to turn the library of *las Descalzas* into a minor gem of learning in the Church's crown. Not only do we gather up and preserve as many of the old manuscripts as we can, but I have given it to be known that any messenger who brings me tidings yet unheard from the New World shall have rewards both spiritual and material. Those who wonder how generous a recompense I can make have only to glimpse the ring I wear. Its rarity of shade alone would make it precious—carbuncles are usually the color of blood, not of heaven—and its size confirms its worth.

I am only guarding it for a friend. She will return for it because she must, because it is her right as well as her legacy, because it signifies the burden of rule she has assumed, because she made a bargain.

Because it is a visible sign of something she already knows with all her heart.

It is for such another sign that I wait here, behind the convent walls; a sign to tell me that she has succeeded in the mission he bequeathed her with his death. Has she found them where they hide, the beings of bright enchantment? Has she coaxed from them the fear that drove them from our midst? Has she taken up the desert prophet's staff in her small, dark hand and led them back into a world made poorer by their absence? That is the news I await.

Instead I entertain a steady stream of greedy wagtongues who elbow each other aside on the road from the port of Seville, trying to be the first to inform me that Pizarro has had Almagro murdered, that Almagro's followers have returned the compliment by killing Pizarro, that Cortés has at last been entombed in the land he conquered. I receive them always in the fountain court.

It is a garden now. Planting it was my first official act as Mother Ana *de las Descalzas*. Flowers invariably do well when they bloom above a bed of ashes.

My messengers always kneel before me where I sit on my favorite bench in the pear tree's shade. When they look up to speak, they must gaze at the statue of that mother and child which is the wonder of our convent. I commissioned it. I paid for it from my own hand. It is a very lovely image, the young woman's face carved to my exact orders. I saw to it that the sculptor received gold enough to tell any who asked that my dictatorial demands sprang from a holy vision of the Virgin Herself, rather than from the quirks of an overripe maidenhead. I paid more to have the mother's billowing robes leafed over with a skin of beaten gold from the mines of New Spain.

(Any of my spiritual daughters unwise enough to remark in my presence upon the similarity between the lady's gilded gown and a *sanbenito* are usually cured by a night's vigil before the image. I have them pray the Office of the Dead. A *sanbenito?* I laugh the idea to tears.)

Today no one shares the pear tree's shade with me. Beside me on the stone bench rest my cup of ink, my spare quills, and the box of tawny red brazilwood which contains the pages that passed beneath my pen so long ago. I have not opened this box—Zamiz' parting gift—until today. I did not truly believe I would ever have cause to add to what already has been written.

Yet today I write. I have taken the ring from my finger, the better to grasp my pen. I will not put it on again. My time of guardianship is done.

Today, just as I was returning from the tedious business

of hearing what stale "news" my visitors might bring, I was accosted by our chief cook, Sister Marta. Her face was red and shiny as a boiled crab, and by the ear she dragged a squirming sprawl of soot-black limbs and squalling lungs.

"Justice, Mother Ana!" she bellowed, giving her prisoner a cuff that pitched him to the ground. He quickly gathered himself into a tight little ball, the better to make himself too small a target for blows. Skinny as he was, I wondered whether the meager creature might not compact himself clean out of existence.

I stooped before him and stroked the matted hair, much to Sister Marta's outrage. "Who are you, my child?" I asked.

Sister Marta supplied one answer: "A graceless orphan brat we took into our house for charity's sake! A thankless bastard whom we should have left in the streets with his worthless friend!"

The child supplied another: "Please, holy mother, my name is Lázaro. My friend's name is Gil, but he—he ran off. We work in the kitchen, turning the spit, tending the ovens, feeding the fires, and cleaning the hearths."

"And what is your crime, Lázaro?" I asked. The child vehemently denied any transgression, either on his part or the absent Gil's. I saw Sister Marta take a deep breath, in preparation for a long rebuttal. I was sure she would vent an endless tale of petty thieveries.

Instead I heard her say, "May God have mercy on his misbegotten soul, but the boy is the filthiest of liars."

"A liar?" I repeated. This I could not believe; the *filthy* part was self-evident.

"All evil springs from falsehood," Sister Marta asserted. "Lies build the walls of hell. This morning I sent the boy and his companion on an errand, to fetch back a box of spices from *don* Jacinto's shop near the docks. It was a task to consume the time it takes to boil asparagus. I told them not to dawdle." She pursed her lips. "They did not return for over two hours."

When I pointed out that this was sloth, not deceit at work, Sister Marta clicked her tongue over my simplicity and added, "But when I demanded to know why they had flaunted me, *then* the lies! Outrageous! Absurd!" Her tiny eyes narrowed still further and looked to blister the child's skin with their wrath. *"Sinful."*

Lázaro clutched at my skirt with one grubby paw. "Please, holy mother, you must believe me. We didn't lie, Gil and I! Sister Marta asked why we were late, and we told her the truth: When we went down to *don* Jacinto's shop by the water, we saw something wonderful. We did! They were right there, between the hulls of two small ships. One of them was playing with the anchor chain. That was why we took so long coming back. We had to stay, to see, to make sure we could believe our own eyes. We looked and looked, until we couldn't doubt it. We swore on the Gospels what we saw was so, but Sister Marta wouldn't listen. She started to whip us. Gil ran away, but he was telling the truth as much as I—"

I took the boy into my arms and hushed his chatter before I asked, "And what was this true thing you saw, my little friend? A pretty fish? A white rat? A seagull the color of gold?"

He opened his eyes wide as the love of heaven and very solemnly said: "We saw mermaids."

So there it is, the sign I have awaited. The merfolk are only the first, the rest will follow. Lázaro has been given a suit of fine clothes, a patrimony from my private sources, to be kept in trust for his manhood, and a letter of instruction to an honest local merchant, explaining why it would profit him to adopt the boy. He has also been given a bath. I hope we may serve Gil likewise. I have the tidings I desired; now let the New World go its ways.

I know that I ought to lay down my pen, for all things are accomplished. I cannot. Though this tale is told and the box beside me brims with all the pages I have already written, I know its secret: There is always a blank sheet awaiting me at the very bottom of the box. No matter how many pages I fill, there is always another. There will always be another, until the day I die. Even then, my soul will cling protesting to my body, clamoring to inscribe the epilogue.

Author's Note

In the diaries of Columbus' first voyage to the New World he wrote: *El dia pasado . . . veíamos sirenas. (Yesterday we saw mermaids.)* These "mermaids" were probably manatees. Considering this, it is no wonder the Admiral of the Ocean-Sea did not find them to be as beautiful as legend promised.